Comments of recovery professionals about this book:

"I loved this book. It is about time the addicted person's intelligence was addressed. The challenge was that I had to reread several paragraphs, stop and THINK which is a significant indicator of my own recovery/discovery of life. It appealed to me on a very personal level. The Post Traumatic Shock Disorder (PTSD) was real to me as a fellow survivor. It helped enormously.

On a professional level, it is a must certainly for those mental health professionals who are not sufficiently aware of addiction . . . and addicts. Who think only of addictions as drug and alcohol. This is a book about challenge. It applies to any recovery. It is for people who want to feel better about life and themselves. It is about discovery of self, of life, of spirituality. It is a voice of the spirit of people and their unrecognized power. In this time of our cultural predeliction to hatred, it is a voice of love and reason, a joyful communicator between East and West. It is a truth of "NO PAIN NO GAIN." Pain is inevitable and suffering is optional. We have choices. I believe my primary mentor, Dr. Viktor Frankl, would have endorsed this book. There were times when I thought of him and "Man's Search for Meaning." I can pay no greater compliment."

—Yvonne Kaye, Ph.D.
Author of *Credit, Cash and Codependency*

"Your book has sharp glimpses of the psychological past and present of the central character . . . *Twelve Steps from the East* is vividly and clearly written, without pretense and with authenticity."

—Myron Sharaf, Ph.D.
Author of *Fury on Earth: A Biography of Reich*

TWELVE STEPS

FROM THE

EAST

BY

RALPH L. BROCKWAY

ASIAN HUMANITIES PRESS

Berkeley, California

ASIAN HUMANITIES PRESS

Asian Humanities Press offers to the specialist and the general reader alike, the best in new translations of major works and significant original contributions, to enhance our understanding of Asian literature, religions, cultures and thought.

Library of Congress Cataloging-in-Publication Data

Brockway, Ralph L., 1926-
  Twelve steps from the East: a novel on recovery and healing / Ralph L. Brockway.
    p.   cm.
  Includes bibliographical references (p.   ).
  ISBN 0-89581-904-X
  I. Title.
PS3552.R6146T94   1992
813'.54—dc20   92-13156
                                              CIP

Copyright © 1992 by Asian Humanities Press. All rights reserved. No part of this book may be reproduced, stored in a retrieval system, or transmitted, in any form or by any means, electronic, mechanical, photocopying, recording or otherwise, without the written permission of the publisher except for brief passages quoted in a review.

To Ann

Table of Contents

Note to Readers	ix
I A Voice in the Head	1
II Where the Action Is	9
III Some Background Music	19
IV The Nightmare	29
V A Game of Chance	39
VI Another Voice Is Heard	49
VII Come Confusion, Come Delusion	68
VIII A Mind-bending Trip	77
IX Doubleheader	94
X The Package	104
XI Talk About Coincidence	115
XII A Sweet Dream	128
P.S. "Lead Me from the Unreal to the Real"	139
Appendix	143
Notes	144

Illustrations

Swami Vivekananda as a wandering monk	86
Rabindranath Tagore	124
Sri Ramakrishna	127
Girish Chandra Gosh	134

Photographs of Swami Vivekananda, Sri Ramakrishna and Girish Chandra Gosh reproduced with permission from *The Gospel of Sri Ramakrishna,* as translated into English by Swami Nikhilananda and published by the Ramakrishna-Vivekananda Center of New York. Copyright 1942 by Swami Nikhilananda; Seventh Printing 1984.

Note to Readers

The setting for this book is a hospital rehabilitation center or unit for the treatment of alcoholism and drug addiction. The hospital is located in a major metropolitan area, and the unit, which is acknowledged as one of the finest on the East Coast, accommodates approximately forty patients, or substance abusers, as they sometimes are called.

The patients are under no restraint to stay once they enter for treatment, and it is not unusual for some of them to walk out soon after they are admitted. Nor is it unusual for some to return sometime after discharge for another round of treatment.

The usual stay is twenty-eight days. Treatment during this time consists of various group therapies, individual consultations with psychiatrists, social workers and other specialists and an educational program about the nature of various addictions. Other than for mood-controlling medication prescribed individually by psychiatrists to give temporary relief, no medicines are available to cure the addictions and prevent the troubles they cause. The only lasting road to recovery prescribed by the medical staff is participation in the Twelve Step Program of Alcoholics Anonymous and Narcotics Anonymous which have chapters just about everywhere in the U.S.

Attendance at six or seven meetings a week of AA or NA or both, depending on the addictions of a patient, is part of the rehabilitation program. These meetings are at various locations in and out of the hospital.

Upon discharge, if the rehabilitated alcoholic or addict cannot find a way to become part of the widespread fellowships of AA and NA, he is left pretty much on his own and in all probability will return to the desperation of his addiction within a short time.

This book addresses some of the beginning difficulties many alcoholics and addicts have in attempting to work their way, as it is called, through the Twelve Steps. Often they are stymied by Steps Two and Three and can get no further because they lack or cannot believe in a higher power, which is the requirement of Step Two. Without this higher power, it's impossible for them to practice Step Three which calls for them to turn their will and lives over to the care of God, as they understand Him. Since these steps are the foundation for all the ones that follow, recovery is severely threatened or at a minimum faces an insufferable, even intolerable delay. In dramatizing this dilemma, this book brings into play advice and support from a source that will be surprising to most readers, the ageless *Bhagavad Gita* and yoga practices of India.

CHAPTER ONE

A Voice in the Head

Charley groaned inwardly and thought: What's all this shit?

He sat in a very nice place. It was like a comfortable old-fashioned country club that had been on the skids for a while. Wide halls and high ceilings. Old English sporting prints on the walls, marble fire places, complete with plush furniture that was beginning to show shabby signs of age and wear.

So what! It was still another fucking rehab center. No disguising that!

Charley was in for dual addiction. Drugs and alcohol. An addict twice-over. A double-dose.

Everyone was nice:
Nurses,
Nurses aides,
Supervisors,
Social workers,
Searchers,
Do-gooders,
Knowers,
Doubters,
Doctors,
Even his psychiatrist at $100 an hour, day after day.

So why shouldn't they be nice? That's what they get paid for, isn't it?

Shit! To put it politely. They don't know their fucking ass from a hole in the ground.

Charley'd about had it. A colossal, aching, ass-busting downer.

Three or was it four times he'd checked into rehabilitation hospitals? Then changed his mind, gotten cold feet and walked right out the door to the nearest bar and from there, to make matters worse, to the nearest street-corner dealer. In one day, out the next. Or once he'd made it a one day round trip, in in the AM and out in the PM. All stupid. All useless. Wasn't modern medicine wonderful? Fuck it!

Where's the cure? God knows I need it. This time I'll just have to stick it out at this place, the whole twenty-eight days, maybe more if it doesn't take hold. My old friend Billy spent three months taking one of these fragile cures and then "went out" again two weeks after discharge. What a mess he was! Shaking, crying, vomiting, hearing voices and going right back into the hospital in a straight jacket. I heard he's doing better and back at work now. If he can do it, maybe I can, but sure as hell not the way I feel now. No way!

Thing is these great minds say addiction is a disease. They even have Blue Cross and the insurance companies believing it. But they offer nothing of their own that really cures and lasts. No discovery. No new wonder drug. No miraculous cure, no balms, not even aspirin.

Just Alcoholics Anonymous or Narcotics Anonymous. Take your pick. One or the other. Or take both. But you gotta get with it, one way or the other. That's it!

They say it's all up to me.

All I have to do is do the Twelve Steps.[1]

Great!

Anyone can do it. Child's play. All you need is a higher power. You turn everything over to it. You don't do it, your higher power does it.

Sounds like an easy out. Let your higher power do it. "Let go, let God," they say. Simple as that and you'll be clean and straight. He'll do it for you.

What a bunch of wishful thinking. Hog wash! As they say down on the farm. A bunch of Sunday school crap!

What higher power? What are they talking about? Where do you find one? Where do you look? Now you see it, now you don't. Can't they do better than that? What am I supposed to do, write a letter?

Dear Higher Power:
Come out, come out, wherever your are. Come out, come out, whoever you are.
Yours truly,
Charley, the recovering addict.

What do the Holy Rollers say? Ask and you shall receive. Well, I'm asking!

God, I sure as hell could use some help. And believe me, not from some fucking religious freak.

Where are you? Who are you? How do I believe in you?

Are you mother, father, lord, master, friend, lover? What the hell are you, anyway?

Let's get with it!

I'm finished. Nowhere to go. Awful. Shitty doesn't even begin to describe how I feel. I'm in the pits. The absolute bottom pits. I've about had it.

So let's hear from this great higher power. Or maybe I'll get it over with on my own. Once and for all!

Charley was exhausted, at the end of his rope. He wasn't sure he wanted to go on. He fell silent, his thoughts still.

Quietly, a voice came from the back of his head. The words had an ancient ring to them. The voice said:

I am the origin and end of the universe.
There exists nothing whatever higher than me. All this, the universe, is strung on me like gems on a string.

Christ! Thought Charley. What's happening? What's this? A voice in my head! Oh shit! Billy heard voices and look what happened to him. Am I headed right for the putrid snake pit of a locked ward? Heaven help me.

The strong, strangely soothing old voice continued:

I am the taste in water, the light in the moon and the

> sun. I am sound in space and manliness in men.
> I am the pure fragrance in earth, the brightness in flames, the life of all beings and the austerity of ascetics.
> Know me to be the eternal seed of all beings. I am the intelligence of the intelligent, the spirit of the spirited. I am the strength of the strong, without desire or passion.
> Whatever exists, pure and beautiful, foul and ugly, or part of both, comes from me alone. These are in me. I am not in them.
> Deluded by these appearances, the whole world does not know me, the Imperishable One beyond them.

Charley was dazzled. Hey! That's beautiful, he thought. Whoever you are, whatever you are, I'm with you! With it, but out of it! I'll buy that any day, sight unseen. That's the way to be if you can manage it. But who the hell can? I'm in it up to my eyeballs and can't get out of it.

The voice paid no attention to Charley's thoughts and softly moved on:

> This divine delusion of mine is extremely difficult to overcome. But those who take refuge in me alone cross over it.
> Those evil-doers who are deluded and dregs of society, whose understanding has been stolen away and who are demoniac in nature, do not worship me.

I've seen plenty of delusion and confusion, but no divine delusion, thought Charley. And I've sure seen the dregs of society. Pushers and users galore. Can I pull myself up and away from them and out of their clutches? I have to, or I won't live long enough to tell about it. Will this strange voice help me out? Is there a chance in a million I could take refuge in it, whatever it is? Or am I in too deep already, too far gone?

The voice made no promises one way or the other:

> Four types of persons worship me: the afflicted, the
> inquiring, those who seek wealth and the wise.
> All these are good, but the wise person is my very Self.
> For being united with me, he dwells in me alone, the
> Supreme Goal.
> After many births, the man of wisdom worships me,
> realizing that I am all that is. Such a great soul is very
> rare.

What's this many births shit? Charley half muttered to himself. I can't handle a day at a time, much less a bunch of lives. I've only one life to live, until someone tells me different. Or is that what's happening?

The voice once again resumed what seemed to be its relentless course:

> Persons whose sense of discrimination has been stolen
> away by desires for this and that worship other gods,
> following rituals appropriate to their nature.
> I give these devotees unshakable devotion to the gods
> they want to worship faithfully.
> Equipped with that faith, the devotee strives to worship
> his favored god and receives the rewards he desires
> ordained by me alone.
> But the rewards which the people of poor understand-
> ing receive are perishable. The worshippers of the
> gods go to them, but my devotees come to me.

Sounds to me as though this old voice offers a better deal than the other gods do, thought Charley. Wonder what he'd offer me on a trade in of this dissipated body, mind and spirit, the old YMCA trinity. Maybe I'm in luck because I don't have any god to begin with. Maybe I can start all over at the top, with the best and greatest of the gods. One god at a time, one life at a time, one day at a time. At this point it's not all that clear to me, but he's got me listening for a change. Let it all hang out. What've I got to lose? Let's hear some more:

> I am veiled by nature which is created by my mysterious energy. I am not manifest to all. This deluded world does not know me who is birthless and changeless.

Charley's mind was churning up a storm. Bet your bottom dollar! I sure don't know you, old voice. But for all I know, you could be birthless and changeless as you say. A while back, you mentioned four kinds of seekers. Could be I'm like one of them, the afflicted, because I may be smart, but I'm certainly not wise, and I sure am addicted; otherwise I wouldn't be in this goddamn country club of a rehab center with all these other poor wretches. And there are no gods I can worship that I know of. It's pretty hard to turn your life over to a wispy voice in your head of a god that you never heard of. Guess that leaves me out of the Twelve Step Program, because God as I understand him in Step Three really doesn't exist for me.

Yet, whoever you are, wherever you're coming from, your words attract me, more than all the dry, sleep-inducing sermons I heard in that musty-smelling church of my childhood. Come to think of it, that old church is no more. Its pompous preachers spoiled Jesus for me with their prejudiced droning of sin, platitudes and threats. And you know what? Their church fell apart right under their very noses. Its congregation withered and died, and my friends, like me, found no lasting belief. Lots of questions, no answers, no faith.

But now I'm hearing a nameless voice, playing like the Pied Piper right out of a fairy tale. Will it lead a stinking, fucking rat like me out of town and right into heaven? Jesus Christ! That'd be something, wouldn't it?

The voice, undisturbed by Charley's wilder and wilder musings and profanity went on:

> I know all the beings which are past and present and which are to come, but no one knows me.
> All beings are deluded at birth by the deceptive dualities born of love and hate.

> But those who do good deeds, whose sins have ended and who are free from the delusions of love and hate, worship me with steadfastness.
> Those who strive for freedom from old age and death by taking refuge in me know the Inner Self and understand action fully.

This is getting heavy, thought Charley. How do you know if your sins have ended, if they ever do? Maybe I should take a closer look at the steps which tell us to make a fearless moral inventory of ourselves, including admitting our wrongs and being willing to have our faults removed. Who knows, I might begin to feel a little better about myself if I could put it down on paper.

And if I could be free of delusions about love and hate, perhaps I'd also be free of delusions about myself. Also, taking refuge in God or our Inner-most Self must be like asking our higher power to remove our shortcomings. Then, if you get that far along, perhaps you can start doing good deeds and making amends to people you've harmed.

The voice, disregarding Charley's floundering attempt at philosophical reasoning, moved toward a conclusion:

> Those who know me and worship me as present in the material and spiritual aspects as well as in sacrificial acts will know me too at the time of death.[2]

Let's stop right there! Charley muttered to himself. His head was about to burst. Enough is enough! A real live voice in my head. I've never heard the likes of it. I can't be imagining it. It says some big things in a way that's new and that appeals to me. Way over my fuzzy, fucked-up head!
Or is it?
I don't know. Christ! I think I'm about to get the shakes. I don't think I can handle any more right now. A voice in my head is hard to take on top of everything else. But one that says he is everything and knows everything but isn't everything

is far out, really far out! Well there you have it. All I needed was a Chinese puzzle like this. My head was bad enough before. Now it's about to split wide open.

I'm dazed as all get out. Give me some room, please give me some room to think about all this. Everything's mixed up, a big witch's brew. Please don't make it any worse.

Charley buried his head in his arms on the table in front of him and closed his eyes. What next he wondered? Strange words whirling about in my head. It's too much for me. Easy does it, Charley. Easy does it. And he dozed off away from his gnawing addictions and the worry of what to do about this mysterious new voice in his head.

CHAPTER TWO

Where the Action Is

It was 5:30 the next morning. Charley had been deep in sleep, no dreams, nothing at all that he could remember. He dimly felt a returning, long-lost sense of peace and well-being. Too early to get up, he thought, as he lay back on the pillows thinking this is too good to last, things are going to get worse before they get better. He thought of the voice in his head and wondered if it had anything to do with this strange sense of peace surrounded, as he was, by the mayhem of this great and renowned rehabilitation center. Memories of the past began to flicker in his mind.

Charley didn't resist. He felt a little detached and watched his thoughts as they passed before him. Memories of his childhood and of his many aunts on his mother's side caught his attention. There had been six of them and two uncles as well living nearby in the smallish midwestern town he'd grown up in. He'd been a favorite of the aunts. They sometimes called him the silent one because he hadn't said a word until he was three, when to the surprise and relief of everyone he began to speak in sentences rather than words.

His mother was the youngest girl and was almost like a daughter to the older aunts, and when his mother had been injured and hospitalized after an automobile accident, they had lavished tender loving care on Charley. He could remember fleeing from an overly strict housekeeper into the arms of Aunt Elsie several blocks away who calmed his sobs and kept him with her until the housekeeper was dismissed and replaced with a Mrs. Kegley, who was pretty nice, as Charley recalled.

Then with something of a shock, Charley began to remember his mother's "nervous breakdown." Her hip had been broken in the automobile accident, and after six weeks in a dismal six bed ward at St. Joseph's Hospital, she had recuperated in a cast at home lying on a cot in what usually was the dining room of the small two bedroom bungalow his parents had built from scratch. He could see the sunlight streaming in through the windows and his mother lying there writing page after page of what his father called "scribblings" on a pad of white, blue-lined paper. Once he sneaked a look at some of the pages. He could still see the writing before his eyes. It was all about God, but it made no sense to him at all. He'd repressed it; he really didn't want to think about it.

Later when the cast was off, he remembered his mother's tears and crying and finding her incoherent, wandering around their small backyard nude and looking white in the moon-lit night. Then in his mind's eye, he could see the tall, sinister-looking, red-bricked sanatorium she had been taken to where, strapped to a table, they had administered torturous electric shock treatments to her. He couldn't remember much else. It was all blanked out and gone, repressed he supposed. Eventually she came home, had another child and was admired and loved by all who knew her, but there never, never was any reference to those horrible days that had just reoccurred to Charley.

But there was more to it than that, thought Charley. Every one of her sisters and brothers had had "nervous breakdowns" in their thirties, although none as heart-breaking as his mother's. He could remember those of Aunt Elsie, Aunt Alice, Aunt Sue, Aunt Mabel, Aunt Laura, Uncle Chuck, Uncle Will. Aunt Nellie's he couldn't remember because she was old enough to be his grandmother. From what he could recall, they mostly seemed to have been depressed. They simply languished at home for several months while the rest of the family nodded knowingly about the "nervous breakdown" that was running its course. Then each of them seemed to recover and return to life without any further fuss or reference to their breakdowns. Aunt Laura became a spiritualist and sometimes seemed a little spooky, but otherwise they all seemed pretty normal, on the surface at least.

How could all of them have had breakdowns wondered Charley? It was a question that often had crossed his mind.

His best guess was that their intelligence had been insulted to the breaking point by the frustrations of the narrow middle-class lives they led. Every one of the siblings was sharp as a tack, highly intelligent, even brilliant, and they were all married to men and women of far less intelligence and imprisoned in a world of domestic chores and physical labors where the highest level of conversation or thought usually was what the weather was going to be like or who was going the win the pennant in the American League.

How about that! Charley suddenly had a surge of wishful thinking and theorized that maybe he was just having a good old-fashioned "nervous breakdown." That would be great compared to the crack-up he was going through. Or, without realizing it, had he had a sort of breakdown that had led to his addictions to alcohol and cocaine? Could he blame it all on his frustrated intelligence? He honestly didn't think so. He really had enjoyed the soaring highs that came with alcohol and coke. But they related more to trying to recreate the wonderful natural highs he had experienced in playing music, in becoming absorbed in books, in pursuing a new interest or a thrilling new friendship. His life had been full of highs of one kind or another, and after his mother had recovered, not very many lows. That is not many lows until the Vietnam War took him into a nightmare of killing and destruction that he'd tried to relieve with more and more pot, coke and alcohol. Those horrors in the line of duty had been a hideous insult to his intelligence. No doubt about that, but like his mother's mental illness, he didn't want to think about it.

Well, thought Charley, trying to get away from his thoughts, there goes that great feeling of peace and well-being that I woke up with. Too much introspection for a coke-crazed head like mine. And I'll hear plenty more from others as the day goes on and becomes more and more shitty. With a grimace Charley got out of bed and started getting ready for the gloomy day ahead.

Charley had begun to shave. Still sort of good-looking, he thought. Even with the ravages of doing coke and booze.

Might be some hope left after all. But he as he shaved, he continued to be haunted by memories of his life, good and bad, that he was going to have to put aside as he pursued the path to recovery. His past—as a talented young musician, as an obedient but sometimes doubting officer in Vietnam, as a fast-rising advertising account executive on the way to fame and fortune—was over and done with, and the future would have to wait. The friends of his recent past—high-flying men and dazzling women from the world of business and fashion, all big consumers—were over and done with, too. Let's face it, his whole world of the past was finished. His whole life was on "hold." It had to be. If it wasn't, it would finish him off in short order. The words of Step One marched relentlessly through his head: We admitted we were powerless over alcohol and drugs—that our lives had become unmanageable. Fucking A right! Charley concurred, I can at least give a big "yes" to that.

The best Charley could say of life this morning was that he was feeling a little better. He had slept well and felt less fractured. Big things come in little packages, he thought, pulling a cliche out of thin air from the hundreds stored away in his brain from the midwestern vernacular of his boyhood.

He looked again at his reflection in the mirror. Man! What a beautiful head! Full of rocks, my folks used to say. Then remembering the mysterious voice of yesterday, he continued thinking, I've heard of people with metal plates in their head receiving radio programs like a crystal set, but that voice in my head was something else! It sure sounded real to me. Big as life. Smooth, aged and mellow, like good old Jack Daniel's whiskey. And here I am in Philadelphia, right smack in the middle of the Institute of Pennsylvania Hospital, the oldest mental hospital in the U.S.A., hearing a voice. Not a good place for that kind of thing. There are plenty of locked wards around here for people with problems like a voice in the head. I'm not going to tell anyone anything about that! But something about that voice out of the past really gave me a nice boost. Pretty good company, but a little off the wall, he thought.

Pretty ridiculous, though. What would high sounding words like that be doing in my confused, aching head? Where could they come from? Almost like poetry. You'd think it could find better places to mess around in. Curious, I think I remember it said something like:

> Those who want freedom from old age and death take refuge in me, their Inner Self, and understand action fully.

How about freedom from drugs and alcohol? Is that part of the deal? Must be. Almost has to be. To be free from old age and death is about as free as you can get.

And so it says it's my Inner Self. My Inner Self? Sounds like that should be my higher power, doesn't it? Com'on you gotta be kidding! I'll really have to let that one sit a while longer and grow a long white beard.

Also, I wonder what it meant about understanding action fully? It must mean understanding how to act. Or who knows, how not to act. Would it have anything to do with the "Let go, let God" or "Let God do it" slogan they keep talking about in AA and NA meetings? What do you say, old-timer? I'm more than a little confused. Can you straighten me out?

Almost, but not quite to Charley's surprise, the voice sounded again in the back of his head:

> O Charley! In days of yore, I spoke of two ways in the world: the path of knowledge for men of contemplation and the path of action for men of action.
> A person does not gain freedom from action merely by refraining from action, nor does one attain perfection through mere renunciation of action.
> No one can stay even for a moment without action. All are driven to work helplessly by the forces of nature.

But he who controls his senses by the mind and engages in the path of action with the organs of action only and without attachment is superior.

What's this controlling the senses and "organs of action" shit, wondered Charley? Does he mean things like taste in the tongue, feel to the touch, smell in the nose, sound through the ears and sight through the eyes? Don't get attached to what you see, taste, smell, hear, touch and so forth? A sure-fire cure for addiction, if you could only do it! He's using a lot of words and phrases that strain my poor head. Try to keep it simple, old-timer.

The voice, indifferent to Charley's plea, continued on its ageless path:

Action is superior to non-action. Even your physical life cannot be maintained without work.
Except for work done as worship, action in this world creates bondage. Therefore act without attachment in the spirit of sacrifice.

Wait a while, old voice, Charley said to himself. You mean to say that everything I do should be a form of worship? A sacrifice to the gods? Why should I do that? It's unheard of in this day and age. Perfectly ridiculous. And anyway, what god would I sacrifice to or worship, when I don't have one that I can call my own?

Without waiting, the voice went on:

Action originates from nature; nature originates from the Imperishable Spirit. Therefore, the all-pervading Spirit is ever present in sacrifice.
The person, O Charley! who does not follow this ordained wheel of action is sinful and addicted to sense-pleasures. He lives in vain.

Charley interrupted again. Addicted to sense-pleasures?

You sure as hell got it right. The fleeting delights and pleasures of coke and alcohol. They got me by the balls and my life is zero, zilch. That's why I'm here. Is it all in vain? Is there any hope, any way out?

Impassive but kindly, the voice rolled on:

> However, for the person who delights in the Self alone, who is happy with the Self and satisfied with it, there remains nothing to be done.
> Therefore perform action always without attachment. Doing work without attachment, a person attains the Supreme Goal.
> Great kings and others gained perfection through work alone. You should engage in action considering the good of humanity.

Be a do-gooder! That takes the cake, Charley almost mocked. Not when most of the ones I've seen are mean and narrow and full of shit. You can almost see it written on their faces. They probably do more harm than good. That's no way for me to go. Yet, on the other hand, if I could just learn to act in the right way, things might fall into place, after all. And who knows, I just might accidentally be of help to another dreary, suffering addict some way or another, if and when I can somehow get a handle on myself.

The voice came again. It seemed soothing and understanding:

> Whatever the best in a society does, the others do.
> Whatever he sets up as a standard, the people imitate.
> O Charley my boy! In all the worlds there is nothing I have to do, nothing that I may seek, nothing that I do not have, yet I am engaged in action.

He's telling me to get with it, get to work, stop moaning and groaning and wanting this and that, reasoned Charley. He's telling me to think only of the work itself and not worry about the pay, let God take care of that. Pitch in and everthing'll be OK. A real positive thinker, like Norman Vincent Peale, if he's still around these days. Wonder if NVP was a member of AA? He'd have made a good one. I don't know that I can swallow all this self-help advice. I keep thinking I'll do it my way. But actually that hasn't been too great an idea in the past. Anyway, I'll listen a little longer, as if I had a choice, that good old voice is unstoppable.

The voice continued on its own detached way, just as Charley had predicted:

> The wise should not unsettle the minds of the ignorant who are attached to action, but should engage them in action by performing all action well, with detachment. The soul which is deluded by the ego regards itself as the doer of works, all of which are being performed by the forces of nature.
> Ascribing all work to me, with the mind dwelling on the Self, act without desire, without a sense of me and mine, and without sorrow.

There it is again! Charley almost shouted out loud. "Ascribing all work to me" sure as hell sounds like the "Let God do it" or the "Let go, let God" slogan that pops up at every substance abuse meeting. They're full of slogans: "Easy does it," "First things first," "Keep it simple," "Listen and learn," "Live and let live," and who knows how many more. Like the signs the Presbyterians used to hang up at summer Bible School back home. Jesus! What's going on in my head? I'm really getting suspicious, probably paranoid. The old voice sounds like an ancient member of AA, before the founders thought of it even. "Let God do it!" "Ascribing all work to me!" Those things are pretty much the same. That's too much, too much for coincidence!

Well, Charley thought, that's all something to shoot for. I'd like to be free from a lot of things, including out of this moth-eaten place. But I'd need a lot of help and practice to learn how to act without desire and without a sense of "that's mine, look at me, see how good I am." What'd happen to my ego, or what's left of it? What'd my psychiatrist think if I lost my ego? That'd really be one for the books. Or is the voice hinting that my ego's the real problem?

Charley interrupted with another thought that had suddenly occurred to him. Without thinking, he found himself talking to the voice in his head: Hold on for a second! How does a person commit sin? Is he driven forcibly to it even against his will?

The voice replied:

> It is desire, it is anger born of the passionate element in nature, insatiable and fierce. Know this to be the enemy here in this world.

Right on! I'll sure buy that, agreed Charley. I know a lot about desire that's insatiable and fierce. That's exactly why I'm here in this fucking old country club of cures, trying to lick addiction before it licks me. Charley wondered, as he had before, can this old voice help me with its wisdom that must come from out of the past, or who knows, from back out of the future?

The voice kept on, unabated:

> As fire is enveloped by smoke, as a mirror is covered by dust, and as an embryo is covered by the womb, in the same manner discrimination is obscured by passion. Wisdom is enveloped by this insatiable desire, the constant foe of the wise.
> The sense-organs, they say, are superior to their objects. Mind is superior to the sense-organs. Intellect is higher than mind, while the Self is superior to intellect. Thus knowing the One beyond the intellect and restraining the self by the Self, slay the redoubtable enemy in the form of desire.[3]

Man oh man! Listen to the way he carries on! Heady stuff, thought Charley—get beyond the mind and the intellect to my Inner-most Self for the cure, the big fix. Would you believe it? A hell of a lot to think about. I have to get to my higher power to get clean, same as in the Twelve Steps. It sort of helps to hear it from someone out of the goddamned all-knowing, well-meaning, soul-saving program.

If you're going to hear voices, this one sure is a humdinger, as they used to say back home. But I've got enough troubles already without trying to figure this one out. Let's put it all on the back burner and let it simmer a bit. Sounds simple, all you have to do is act without desire and you're on your way to the best of all possible worlds. That voice can talk until it's blue in the face, but it'll never convince me any of this is easy to put into practice. All great things are simple, they say, but I sure wonder where all this funny stuff is coming from. It's a mystery to me. It's a real "Who done it?" or better yet, "Who said it?"

Charley finished shaving, made a face at himself in the mirror, then managed a weak smile and set off without much enthusiasm for his day of lectures, films, addiction meetings and listening to the wails and woes of his fellow addicts in the rehab unit. It could be worse, he thought to himself. Much worse! Here we go. One foot in front of the other. One step at a time, one day at a time—and I almost forgot, one life at a time.

CHAPTER THREE

Some Background Music

Charley's old friend Billy had come down from New York City at the request of Dr. Shaw, the psychiatrist assigned to Charley at the Strecker Rehabilitation Unit of the Institute. Dr. Shaw had asked Charley if there was someone he could talk to who could give him an independent perspective on his somewhat reluctant, uncommunicative new patient. Charley had suggested Billy, saying that at this point in his life Billy probably knew more about him than anyone else around.

Billy had arrived early enough to mess around with Charley a little and have lunch with him in the small restaurant facing the huge walled-in quadrangle that was part of the grounds of the old hospital. After greeting each other with a hug and long-time affection, there hadn't been too much to say. Billy wasn't surprised. He was a recovering addict himself and knew what a devastating situation it was to find yourself trying to get out of what often seemed a hopeless morass of anger, pain and depression.

So they did the best they could, played a sloppy game of backgammon, shot a game of pool which Charley managed to win at the last moment in a sudden surge of concentration and walked around the quadrangle half-a-dozen times observing some of the other walkers, mostly inmates from other units of the hospital, and one nurse walking at a furious pace apparently trying to free herself from some of the stress that must hit, hurt and drain professionals working day-in, day-out with mental patients.

After an unhealthy, but delicious lunch of Philadelphia cheese steaks with fried onions, sliced tomatoes, shredded lettuce, pickles, hot peppers and mayonnaise followed by cigarettes with coffee, they had said a reluctant good-bye with Billy saying he would keep in touch and hoped to see Charley back in New York when he could handle it, that is, assuming Billy could keep on handling it, because you never know when the next slip is coming, do you?

Billy was now sitting in a comfortable leather chair facing Dr. Shaw in his office. Dr. Shaw was a neatly dressed, slightly plump man in his mid-fifties with a Phi Beta Kappa key dangling on a gold chain crossing his vest. He had pink cheeks and clear, light-blue eyes. He looked mentally sharp and intelligent, but also quite conservative. Billy wondered how good a match he would be for Charley who could be a bit on the wild side, but he dropped the thought with the inward conclusion that he must be good or he wouldn't be working here with some of the best in the business.

Dr. Shaw cleared his throat and said, "Thank you for making the long trip here to talk to me Billy, if I may call you that in the first name only spirit of AA and NA. I hope you don't mind, Charley did tell me that you're also a recovering addict, and I wish you the best of success.

"As you may have noticed, Charley isn't doing a whole lot of talking at this stage of his recovery, and sometimes it's extremely helpful to us in treating someone like Charley to talk to a family member or close friend who has had a long-standing relationship with the patient and who can give us some insight into the past. Since Charley suggested that our talk might be helpful, please make yourself comfortable, smoke if you like, and tell me what you can in good conscience about our friend."

Billy lit a cigarette saying, "This is another habit I wish I could kick. Maybe tomorrow, not today.

"Let me see, Dr. Shaw. I guess the best way to begin is to begin at the beginning, as they say.

"Charley and I have been friends, often best of friends, since my sophomore year in high school. That's sixteen or seventeen years ago. We both played in the school band. I was first chair in the flute section. Charley played a lousy clarinet in the last row of the clarinet section; he claimed he never learned how to tongue the instrument. We became fast friends and did a lot of things together, even discovered we were distant cousins on his father's side. He liked music and movies, and although he wasn't a very good clarinet player, he was something of an original on the piano. Here again, he was a little short on technique, but he had a lot of talent, enough so that he was playing professionally in small combos and sometimes even solo in bars and saloons around town during weekends. He said he'd taken two lessons in harmony and from then on could hear the chords coming in his head. He didn't drink, smoke or even swear much at that time, and would often get so absorbed in his thoughts that he didn't see people in the halls when he passed them which made some of us think he was a little 'different.'

"From time to time, he would go on reading binges and almost disappear from the school scene, and once after taking IQ tests, I remember overhearing teachers in the hall talking about him, saying that he had an astonishingly high IQ of 140. He never seemed to study much and was never an honor roll student, but the teachers always seemed interested in him, maybe sensing the potential he had.

"I know that he got wildly interested in chemistry shortly after we met, thinking that it explained how things acted and reacted. One of the chemistry teachers took him under his wing, and by the time he was a junior in high school, he was sitting in on junior college classes. He claimed he was a "victim of a Gilbert Chemistry Set" that he got for a Christmas present, but it paid off with a scholarship to the University of Iowa when he finished high school.

"I think it might be fair to say that Charley always wanted to be accepted by others as a member of the group but nevertheless it always was pretty evident that something set him apart. Later on in college, when he began to drink and smoke cigarettes and pot—heavily at times—I think some of it was because he wanted to be one of the boys and that was something they could accept.

"I was a semester behind Charley and visited him at the University a couple of times, eventually following him there. By the time I arrived, he'd already become something of a

BMOC because of his piano playing. He had a program called "Melodic Moods" a couple of times a week on the college radio/TV station, and a flock of sorority girls had formed a Charley Fan Club and sent him sort of groupie mail and requests at the station.

"Strange, I recall that he never rehearsed for those programs. He'd simply make a list on a little piece of paper of song titles, go to the studio, sit down and play in a semi-darkened atmosphere, occasionally singing a song or two in a shy, soft manner, until he had about thirty seconds left, when he'd break into his theme which was an oldie called "The Dreamer." It was a popular program with farmer's wives all over Iowa. Charley was something of a local celebrity.

"As you might begin to suspect, Charley's pursuit of chemistry was beginning to lag by the end of his sophomore year. I think he told me that organic chemistry finally did him in, although he still had close to a B average. I know that the only time he would really crack a book was the night before a test, when he'd go through the text and decide what the professor was going to ask. The next day he'd go to the exam, quickly write out his answers, and right or wrong be the first to leave. He wasn't above peeking over a shoulder to get a clue, but that was usually all he needed. He told me he could see the textbook page before his eyes, I guess a little like hearing chords, and would just write away as fast as he could before he lost it. Later on when I worked with him in New York in the advertising business, clients would be amazed at how quickly he could learn and seemingly understand their businesses. It was always easy for him and hard for me. We both ended up on alcohol and drugs, so I don't know that one way is better than the other.

"Sorry, Dr. Shaw, I digressed a little, but not very far. At the end of his sophomore year, Charley took some recordings of a college combo he'd been playing with into one of the big booking agencies in Chicago and managed to get the group booked for the summer into a resort high up in the

Rockies. It may have been near Reno, I'm not sure. That was the last I saw of Charley for a good long while. He loved the thrills of playing to an audience and dropped out of college to play for a year or two, or who knows how long. Charley said he'd be back to finish up, but I'm not sure he really meant it.

"One thing he forgot about, however, was the Vietnam War which was getting underway, and before he knew what had happened I think he found himself in the army getting trained for action. He was spotted for officer's training, commissioned and shipped off to Vietnam in plenty of time to see what must have been some really nasty action, although I'm guessing some here because he's never talked about it to me, and I've sensed he doesn't want to because it's painful to him. I do know that he returned a well-seasoned user of cocaine in addition to his by now well established use of alcohol and pot.

"We'd kept in touch from time to time, and I had my BA in liberal arts and was slowly working my way up the ladder as an account executive in a New York advertising agency when Charley called and said he was out of the army and looking for work doing something with more of a future than hacking around the world of music. We got together again and I helped Charley get a start at my agency as an assistant account executive. Well, as you can probably guess by now, Charley has sort of a golden touch, and before you knew it he was an account executive and within less than two years a supervisor with a sure ticket for vice president if he kept his nose clean, which, pardon the pun, he obviously didn't do. The clients liked him because he came up time after time with ideas that they had vaguely in the back of their heads but couldn't express or articulate. Charley seemed almost to read their minds, and he had an incredible sense of timing that left some of us who were less talented open-eyed as he passed us by on the way up the corporate totem pole.

"At that point, Charley and I more or less lost contact, not that we didn't see each other. He was leading a pretty fast, high life, entertaining clients, engineering big deals and making very good money. I was left in the dust, so to speak, like the slow, plodding tortoise in the hare and the tortoise fable.

"To make matters worse, I had been living with a great girl for several months, and she left me to go with Charley.

"I began to sink in my own world of coke and booze and loneliness as Charley seemed to fly away seemingly unharmed and successful in his. Matters went from bad to worse for me, and I ended up a sad sack in and out of the Goodman Clinic in Scarsdale several times. By the time I got a hold on myself and made it back into the world with a lot of help and support from AA and NA and some of the people I used to work with, Charley had taken his own nose dive during a business trip here to Philly.

"Somehow or other, probably with help from one of his clients, he got himself admitted here and finally seems to admit that he needs help. I hope he can accept it. I hope you can find a way to give it to him. I wish him all the best. No bitterness. He's still my friend. What else can I tell you Dr. Shaw?"

Dr. Shaw had been writing in a black leather journal, taking notes in what appeared to be a small, meticulous hand. He looked up, paused, then said, "You mentioned, Billy, that Charley took up with your girl. What else can you tell me that might be pertinent about his likes or preferences for one sex or the other?"

"That's a tough question to ask a friend," said Billy. "But as a friend, if there's a chance it might help Charley's recovery, I'll answer as best I can."

Billy stopped to think for a moment, then continued, "Women, old and young, seem to like Charley and in a way make a pet of him. I don't think Charley objects to this. His affair with my friend Nellie lasted several months until Charley's habits made their life together impossible. This is the only prolonged affair that I'm aware of. Otherwise he played the singles game in Manhattan and dated a number of very attractive women on a catch as catch can basis. I met many of them, a little hard and calculating, but nice enough for a short-term relationship.

"I know next to nothing of what happened in Vietnam, or when he was traveling around the music circuit, but in both college and high school I'm unaware of any big romances or live-in arrangements. He went out with girls, we used to double-date occasionally, but not on any kind of a steady basis. You have to remember that most week-ends he was playing in combos or bands which put him on a different track from the rest of us.

"I think he's pretty straight about sex," said Billy. "I can remember a physical attraction between us when we were friends in high school, but no overtures were made and nothing ever came of it. I think he likes men but prefers women. If he's played both sides of the street at one time or another, it's not obvious to me, and it wouldn't really make much difference anyway in this day and age." Billy gave a nervous shrug and shifted in his chair, indicating he was finished on the subject of sex.

"That's helpful, Billy," said Dr. Shaw understandingly. "Now, if you could tell me what you remember of Charley's family and home we should be about finished. You've been very patient with my questions."

"That's a much easier question," said Billy smiling again. "I used to stop by fairly often, and they treated me like a visiting cousin. We lived in Yellow Springs, Ohio, a small midwestern town with mostly narrow ideas, although Antioch College is located there and offers a liberal refuge if anyone wants it. Charley's father was a machinist in a nearby oil refinery. He didn't make a lot of money, but there was enough for a modest, comfortable life. Charley's mother was bright and pert and kept you on your toes when talking to you. She was very direct, almost to the point of being rude at times, and seemed to have little sense of ego. She was lame, I think from a broken hip in an automobile accident, and I gather from remarks Charley made, had been seriously ill over a period of time that included the birth of Charley's sister who was ten or eleven years younger than Charley. I remember Charley saying that he practically raised his sister during his mother's illness. I know they were very close. I didn't see all that much of Charley's father, but I recall that he smiled often, asked what I thought of the Indian's chances for the pennant but otherwise didn't seem all that much at ease talking to me. He was nice enough, but not nearly as memorable as Charley's mother.

"I guess you could say they were a fairly typical, middle-class WASPish family with plenty of the race and religious prejudices you'll find in melting pots like Yellow Springs. And oh yes, one other funny sort of thing, the family were teetotalers, didn't even drink beer or wine. Of course they didn't eat spaghetti or use garlic either. Anyway, Charley used to get a sardonic glint in his eye and tell of playing in the cocktail lounge of one of the local hotels while his mother was attending a meeting of the local WCTU across the hall."

"Thank you Billy," said Dr. Shaw, "that kind of background is pertinent and good to know. Is there anything else you can dredge up in the few minutes we have left that might help me work with Charley?"

Billy thought for a few seconds, then said rather dubiously, "There is one thing a little on the weird side that happened a few months after Charley began working at the agency.

"Charley had never been very religious. Actually he was very turned off, I think, by the small-town Presbyterianism his parents followed, but I think he had some kind of religious bent in the back of his head that had been at work for quite a while. He may have been what some people might call a secret seeker.

"I don't know what made this happen. Charley may have gotten into Eastern thought when he was in Vietnam, or possibly he was having problems with his conscience over what he'd done or ordered his soldiers to do over there, but anyway, one day he emerged from a three day party with hardly a trace of a hangover and a new philosophical or religious theory or system that he called 'The Curves'. As best I can recall from the foggy past, there was a three-dimensional curve for every area of human endeavor, with an axis each for knowledge, understanding and happiness. All these curves had a common focal or end point, and everyone was on them. If anyone reached the top of a curve, he found total happiness and God. Or he may have become God-like, I'm not clear on that. He also said that people were drawn up these curves by the magnet of their own potential, and that when they stopped trying to ascend them, they fell back, lost happiness and understanding and became shallow, disappointed shells of themselves.

"Come to think of it, he may have been trying to explain things that happened in his own family, because I had the feeling that his mother had a lot of intelligence she wasn't putting to use. Hard to tell. Anyway, Charley talked about these curves to anyone who would listen for weeks on end, threatening to become a total bore. Finally I think the system got so complex and impossible to explain that Charley had to give up on it. I know it got pretty hard to follow, to put it politely, when he was drinking, which was more often than not. The last I can remember was that he announced he needed a fourth dimension to make it work, and even then he wasn't sure he'd be able to explain it. Could be that Charley started to slip down his own curve. He may even have fallen off it, who knows.

"I suppose you have lots of people in this place with nutty theories about God, but I never thought Charley's approach was all that nutty. It made a certain amount of sense, and you have to give him credit for at least trying to sort things out."

Billy glanced quickly at his watch. "I'm sorry, Dr. Shaw, I'm going to have to run. My train back to the City leaves in twenty-five minutes. I hope this helps. In a way it's helped me to be able to feel that I might be of help to Charley. We've had our ins and outs, ups and downs, but he's still a friend in my book, and they're hard to come by. Incidentally, speaking of ins and outs, Nellie and I have gotten back together again. I guess you'd call it a *menage a trois* in French Literature 101. I didn't say anything about it to Charley, but somehow, I don't think it would upset him greatly."

"You've been very informative, Billy," said Dr. Shaw. "Charley is an interesting, complex and possibly brilliant man with some awesome addictions. What you've told me may help me communicate better with him. You're a good friend, Billy, and I wish you well on your own road to recovery. Again, my thanks for your help."

The two men rose, shook hands, and Billy left with a warm feeling of having done something worth doing during his day in Philadelphia.

CHAPTER FOUR

The Nightmare

It was early, 6:15 in the AM. Charley wasn't sure he could make it out of bed. He'd just waked up. He was in a cold sweat. His pajamas were damp. He'd had a crazy dream, a horrifying nightmare. He couldn't forget it. He could see it again rolling in like a cloud of hot, misty fog and materializing before his eyes:

He was back in Vietnam, in the hot, steaming jungle, a kid with first lieutenant's bars leading a platoon of weary, sweat-stained soldiers stumbling along an overgrown path. You could almost feel their mortal fear in the heavy moisture-laden air.

Their orders were to retake a lousy hill. It meant risking death to kill and maim other human beings. Was it worth it? What fucking good would it do? A lot of people had doubts about this war. But Charley kept telling himself that he didn't. He had to believe. He couldn't have doubts and still lead men into battle. For Charley, the war had to be righteous and for the good of his country and the whole wide world. You'd better bet your ass on it. And sometimes, if doubts did begin to seep and creep through his belief, a hit of pot or dope gave him the boost he needed to go on strong and fortified for a while, if not for long.

Charley sighed, the outline of the hill was in sight now. He was tired and frightened, wished he were back home again in Ohio, or playing piano in a bar, or anywhere but here. He'd have to deploy his men soon for the attack. Dismayed and resigned, he took out his field glasses for a closer look. Oh fuck! What the shit was this? Someone must have messed around with his glasses. He could see everything! Even the faces of the slant-eyed enemy, alert and waiting in their hidden hill-side positions. Funny how they all still looked alike to him. One round, yellow face fit all.

But that wasn't all. Suddenly, the faces had changed! Instead of orientals, all strangers, all looking the same, Charley saw his own grandfathers, uncles, teachers, cousins and friends, all near and dear to him. And all ready for bloody battle, waiting to kill or be killed.

He couldn't believe it! His orders were to take the hill and in so doing he would have to assault and fight to the death his own kith and kin. What a horrendous, shattering, disastrous topsy-turvy dilemma. It was totally unreal, but there it was real and unchanging right before his eyes, a nightmare he couldn't shatter.

Charley had tried to stop the dream, but he was trapped and couldn't escape. He was overwhelmed with great pity and sorrow, for himself and for those he was about to fight to the death.

He was flooded with thoughts in a manner unfamiliar to him. What the hell was this? His thoughts seemed to come from the same day and age in the same manner as the words of that ancient voice he'd been hearing. Charley heard himself say:

> O Lord! Seeing my own people assembled here to
> fight, my limbs are weary and my mouth is drying up.
> My body trembles and my hair is standing on end. My
> weapons are falling away, and my skin is burning.
> I am unable to remain steady and my mind is wandering
> —and I see evil omens.
> God! I do not see any good in killing my own friends
> and family in war. I do not desire victory, nor medals,
> nor the pleasures of winning.
> These I do not want to kill, even for the sake of ruling
> over all the worlds, not to speak of this earth alone.
> Alas, what a great sin we have set ourselves to commit
> as we have become ready to kill our own people out of
> greed for the pleasure of victory.
> I think it will be better for me if my relatives kill me
> unresisting and unarmed.[1]

The Nightmare

Exhausted by this awesome conflict, Charley, with mind laden with grief, sank down against a tree trunk in the stinking, steaming jungle overwhelmed with pity and with eyes full of tears.

Firmly and with compassion the ancient quiet voice had sounded in the back of his head saying:

> O Charley! Whence has this delusion come over you at the moment of crisis? This is unworthy of a brave man. It does not lead to heaven and is disgraceful.
> O My Young Friend! Do not give way to unmanliness. It does not befit you. Discard this petty weakness of heart and arise, O Destroyer of Enemies!

Charley had responded, speaking again in the strange, ancient and archaic manner:

> How can I, O Ancient Voice! fight brothers and teachers with bullets and flaming explosives in this war? They are worthy of my worship.
> It is better to live in the world by begging than to slay these venerable beings. By slaying them I will only taste pleasures of victory stained with blood.
> Nor do I know which is better—whether we conquer them or they conquer us. My friends and family, after slaying whom I would not care to live, I see confronting us here.
> I do not perceive anything which will allay this sense of withering grief even if I obtain dominion over earth without an enemy or even sovereignty over gods in heaven.

Having thus spoken, Charley declared to the voice:

> I will not fight, and became silent.

The ancient voice spoke these words to Charley who was

grieving and powerless in the dark, dank jungle:

> You are lamenting for those for whom there should not be any lament; yet you speak words of wisdom. The wise do not grieve for the dead or the living.
> Never was a time when you or I or your family and friends did not exist; nor will any of us cease to exist afterwards.
> As childhood, youth and old age are to the indwelling spirit in the body, so also is its migration to another body. The wise have no delusions about it.

Jesus! Was the voice telling me that you can't really kill anyone? It's all pre-ordained? Everyone simply goes on to another life, queried Charley, half in and half out of his nightmare. No guilt, no grief as long as it's right action. Nothing to harm. That's too easy, too good to be true. Sure wish I could believe it. Problem is, who's to say it's right action?

The voice had gone on its inscrutable way:

> Sense-contacts give rise to feelings of heat and cold, pleasure and pain. They come and go and do not last forever. Endure them.

Was he telling me nothing lasts forever, thought Charley? That's good to hear because I'm not sure sometimes if the pangs of war and pains of addiction will ever let up. It feels like they're going to last forever. Can you tell me how to get beyond them, old friend?

The voice had seemed soothing and reassuring as it continued on:

> He who is unaffected by these dualities and who is the same in pleasure and pain deserves eternal life.
> Know that which pervades all this is indestructible. No one can destroy the Eternal Spirit.

> These bodies of the incarnated Spirit, which is eternal, indestructible and imperceptible, have been declared to be perishable. Therefore, O Young Warrior! fight.
> How can he who knows this to be imperishable, eternal, birthless and changeless, slay anyone or cause anyone to slay?
> As a man puts on new clothes after discarding the old ones, so also does the embodied spirit enter into new bodies after giving up the old ones.

Charley, still recollecting his dream, but by this time feeling more awake and like his old familiar self, began to go over again in his mind what the voice had been saying. He's been talking a lot about rebirth, that the soul is born over and over again but the pure inner Self remains untouched and free forever.

If I heard him correctly, as long as I acted in the right manner, I shouldn't feel guilty about those poor Vietnamese I may have killed or about those buddies of mine who were killed under my command because it's impossible to kill anyone and they're already on their way to another body, more than likely for another round of misery and suffering. Goodness knows, I'd like to believe it all couldn't be helped and feel that my conscience is free and clear.

You know, all of this must be something like karma and reincarnation, but I don't know much about either, barely heard of them. I don't think my voice is coming from this part of the world, but if what it says is true, I might have a glimmer of hope of doing better next time around, and life here and now might seem more worth the effort. I wish it all were clearer.

Compassionately, the ancient voice began to speak again in his head:

> Weapons cannot sunder it, nor fire burn it. Water cannot wet it, nor the wind dry it.
> The Spirit which dwells in all bodies is eternal and can

never be slain. O Charley! You should not therefore grieve for anyone.

That's easier said than done, thought Charley. It's a blue sky approach if I ever heard one. I can sort of see it, but I don't think I'd ever be up to hurting or killing someone without feeling bad about it. Or for that matter, I can't imagine not grieving over the death of my mother or father.
The voice kept on with its advices:

Even considering your duty as a leader of men, you should not waver, for there is no higher good for a warrior than a righteous fight.
Now if you do not fight this battle, you will incur sin for relinquishing your duty and honor.
If you are slain in battle you will go to heaven, and if you win you will enjoy victory and acclaim. Therefore arise, resolved to fight.

Holy Christ in Heaven! exclaimed Charley to himself, recalling for a moment the rolling oaths of friends from Irish and Italian Catholic families of his boyhood in Ohio. After all those high-sounding words about acting without desire, now he's trying to ply me with rewards of heaven, victory and honors. He uses every argument in the books, and then some, to convince me that to fight is right. That old magician just doesn't give up. He sure puts up a good argument for fighting. You can't lose, six of one, half-a-dozen of the other. Be a better bargain for me if I only believed in heaven. What do you say, old friend, can you sweeten the offer?
The magical sounding voice seemed to promise more:

Treating alike pleasure and pain, gain and loss, victory and defeat, get ready to fight. Acting thus you will not incur sin.
This is my ancient wisdom which has been imparted to you, O Inquiring Friend! Now listen to my under-

The Nightmare

standing, equipped with which you will cut the bondage of action.
In this path no effort is lost and no fault is committed.
Even a little of this practice saves one from great fear.
You have the right to action alone, never to its results.
Do not desire results of action nor be attached to non-action.
Being the same in success and failure, work without attachment, for evenness of mind brings freedom from bondage.
A person of understanding becomes free from good and evil even in this life. So practice this understanding; understanding is skill in action.

Aha! thought Charley. Skill in action must be like knowing how to turn everything over to God. If you do it right, you can't do anything wrong, I guess even if it means killing an enemy or getting killed in a so-called righteous war. But it's hard to do things right when your mind and practically everything else has been stolen away by cocaine and drink. No doubt about it! That's why I'm in this old hospital, listening to a lot of toothbrush-clean evangelicals tell me how to get straight and hearing this ancient old voice speak a lot of words that are sure as hell time-warped. But nevertheless, some of what he says hits home like nothing I've ever heard before.

The voice explained further about action:

Renouncing the results of action, wise persons of understanding become free from the bondage of rebirth and gain the untroubled state.
When your understanding overcomes your turbid delusion, then you will be indifferent to what has been heard or what is to be heard.

A question popped into Charley's mind about this rare state of understanding. He wondered:

What are the marks of a person of steady wisdom who is established in the Self? How does a person of steady understanding speak? How does he dwell, and how does he conduct himself?

The voice spoke:

When, O Charley! a person gives up all the desires of mind and finds pleasure in the Self by the Self, he is said to be steady in wisdom.
One who is unworried amid sorrows, desireless amid pleasures and who is without attachment, fear or anger is said to be a person of stable understanding.
When a person withdraws the senses altogether from their objects just as a tortoise draws its limbs inward, then his wisdom is steady.

I feel like that turtle sometimes when I simply crawl into the fetal position and hope that all my miseries will go away, interspersed Charley. I try to get all the way back into the womb to get away from those craving, powerful senses.
The voice seemed sympathetic as it resumed:

Objects recede from an individual who starves the senses even though there is no loss of craving for them, but even the craving is lost when the Supreme Self is known.
Dwelling on sense-objects a person becomes attached to them. From attachment comes desire, from desire anger, from anger delusion, from delusion loss of memory, from loss of memory comes loss of understanding, and from loss of understanding he perishes.

Some of the things that old voice says really get through to me thought Charley. When I'm on coke and drinking a lot, it doesn't take much to get me raging mad, and when that happens I go way off the deep end, say things I don't mean, hurt people and break up the world around me. Next day I wake up cold sober, hurting, crushed and crashed. Sometimes I sure as hell feel like jumping out the window. It wouldn't take much to push me over and out. Matter of fact, one of my friends did just that. He ended up in a wheel chair paralyzed for life. Another OD'd and wound up in the emergency room of N.Y. Hospital with a brain hemorrhage. He died. And Billy's friend George slashed both wrists and set his house on fire. I hear he's making it back. It's a real ugly scene, real ugly. I hope those times are over and gone for me.

The voice seemed to offer a solution:

But a disciplined individual whose senses roam under control among the objects of sense, free from both attachment or aversion, attains peace of mind.
All his sorrows end upon attaining peace of mind, for the understanding of a peaceful mind becomes steady quickly.
But among the roving senses, the one which the mind follows steals away the understanding of a person just as the wind sets a boat adrift in waters.

That happens to me all the time, Charley thought. No sooner do I think I'll be OK than, oh shit! the urge sneaks up on me and I have to go out and have a drink or a snort of coke and the whole mess starts right over again.

The voice continued to speak about desires:

Just as the ocean stands still like a rock though waters flow into it, even so the person in whom all desires get lost attains peace, not so the desirer of desires.
Giving up all desires, the person who lives without a craving and without a sense of me and mine attains eternal peace.
This, O Charley! is called poise in the Self. No one who gains this is ever deluded. Even if one attains this understanding at death, he gains eternal life.[2]

Slowly Charley returned to the awakening world around him and began to gather his thoughts for the long day ahead. His head felt a little light, and he sensed a slight glimmer or glow. A nice and hopeful feeling for a change.

Would the words of the voice that seemed to come from another time, yet sounded as though it might be timeless ease his conscience about the horrors of killings and destruction in Vietnam that kept haunting his thoughts? He hoped so, but he didn't know. It was a lot to ask, and nothing happened overnight.

But in a way, what had started out as an incredible, inescapable nightmare had left him feeling cleansed, balanced and more ready for the future, or at least for the day ahead. Charley put both feet on the floor and got out of bed feeling he might just do things a little better today.

CHAPTER FIVE

A Game of Chance

Charley was loafing around the rehab quarters between addiction sessions. He was knocking a few balls about on the massive old-fashioned pool table centered in a wide corridor of the old building. He was feeling relaxed, that is for the state he was in and for being where he was, and somewhat fortified. What the hell! At least he had a voice of his own to listen to, not somebody else's higher power to scrape and bow to in fear and awe and cry for mercy. Not for him. He couldn't do that, no matter what! He even had trouble joining hands at the end of meetings to repeat the Lord's Prayer. The prayer itself was OK, but he resented the assumption on the part of the AA and NA chapters that he was a Christian and accepted it. He remained silent throughout in a state of irate rebellion. Any good that the ritual might have offered was lost.

As he racked up the balls, centered them on the table and prepared to break them with the cue ball, Charley's thoughts reverted to his session yesterday with his psychiatrist, Howard Shaw, M.D., who had been assigned to him as part of the recovery program in the Strecker Rehabilitation Unit at the Institute of Pennsylvania Hospital. It had been an unusual session because Charley had said much more than he had intended to, and he had said it better than he thought he could at this early, shaky stage of recovery.

Charley could recall the exchange with Dr. Shaw almost word for word. Dr. Shaw had been looking his dapper best, dressed in a charcoal-grey suit, white oxford shirt with button-down collars and dark maroon club tie with narrow blue and white stripes. White shirt cuffs with round, antique gold links shot neatly one-half inch out of his jacket sleeves, and a white handkerchief was carefully folded to peek out of his breast pocket. His thinning hair had been brushed against his scalp with a precise part, and his black shoes shining against long black socks had been freshly polished.

Charley had appraised the doctor with a jaundiced eye, thinking that he looked like a dandy right out of the sixties. Did he wear a bowler hat? A Brooks Brothers topcoat with an elegant patch of velvet around the back collar?

"How are things with you today, Charley?" Dr. Shaw had asked pleasantly for openers.

"Not bad, Dr. Shaw," Charley had replied, letting the limp exchange lapse into a flat, dead silence.

Not unused to patients with their guard up, Dr. Shaw had taken a deep breath, smiled gently, and decided on his approach for the day. "I had a very good talk with your friend Billy yesterday," he said. "Billy mentioned that at one time you developed a kind of philosophical system that you called 'The Curves'. What little he could tell me about it sounded as though it probably was a serious effort on your part to understand yourself and the world around you. This is a fairly unusual kind of effort, at least for it to reach the stage where you could try to present your thinking as a system and talk about it to others. It might be helpful if you could tell me how it came about and what it was."

Reluctant though he was, Charley had felt himself respond in a positive way to the Doctor's friendly question. Besides, he was still fond of 'The Curves', even though they were hopelessly confused and muddled in his mind.

Charley had looked up, shrugged his shoulders and raised his eyebrows, then said, "I haven't talked about them in a long time, Dr. Shaw, and the system, if it was one, ended up so full of loop holes and impossible paradoxes that I gave up on it, gave myself "A" for effort and went on with my life in pursuit of pleasure and power, to use a polite phrase for it. However, maybe if I tell you a little about how it came about, enough of it will come back to mind to give you an idea or hint of it that might be helpful.

"This happened a couple of years ago. I was stranded in Philly on a business trip with nothing to do for an evening. My clients were all busy elsewhere, and there was no one to entertain except myself. I had noticed in the paper that a revival of

T. S. Eliot's *The Cocktail Party* was playing at the Walnut Street Theater. I thought I'd take it easy for a change and give culture a fling. So I had more than a few drinks and a four star dinner at Le Bec Fin, walked a few blocks to the theatre and settled down into a good last minute seat in the eighth row center.

"The plot is a little muddy in my mind, but I think there were a lot of sophisticated people standing around talking about the usual shallow, everyday things and drinking copiously at a cocktail party, if you know what I mean. Well, one of them got bored with what was going on and, smashed though she was, began to realize how utterly stupid and meaningless all this was and that they were all wasting their lives away day after day. Somehow or other in the midst of this alcoholic haze she actually got inspired to do something about it, and ended up taking a blind journey to the East. The way I recall it, she goes to an island as a nurse of mercy to help the natives; instead, the natives crucify her and then, paradoxically, proceed to worship her as a saint. At the end of the play, those at the original party are together again and hear this shocking news. It means different things to each of them but seems to boil down to something like every moment is a fresh beginning, and they go their separate ways in search of renewed meaning and purpose in their lives.

"Well, I'll be damned! Now that I think about the ending, it sounds awfully close to the slogan I keep hearing at Twelve Step meetings. I think it goes "Today is the first day of the rest of my life," or something to that effect. They sure love slogans. "KISS" I've heard some of them say—"Keep It Simple Stupid."

"Anyway, I guess the parallel between the characters in the play and my own life really hit home to me, and I left the play as inspired as the characters who had set off for points unknown to renew themselves and their lives.

"As I walked into the theater foyer and out into the street, I couldn't believe my ears listening to the chatter of the departing audience around me. They were talking about this joke or that and what a delightful comedy it had been; or some were complaining that it hadn't been as entertaining as *Cats*, the hit musical that had been based on some of TS's poems. It struck me that they had totally missed the point and were as shallow as the people at the party in the beginning of the play.

"I jotted down some notes in my hotel room that night. It seemed to me the characters were seeking happiness or love, I couldn't quite separate one from the other, and that they needed understanding and knowledge to find it. It was also clear to me that knowledge wasn't enough because all the facts in the world are no good if you don't understand how to use them. Finally my writing got too sloppy to read because I was sipping whiskey as I wrote, and I lost my focus and slipped off to bed and sleep.

"Then the next day, I more or less forgot about the whole thing, and I went about business as usual until several weeks later I found myself at what amounted to a three-day cocktail party out in the Hamptons on Long Island. After the second day of silliness and nonsense, I got fed up with the whole scene and retired to my room to pout and stew and wish I were somewhere else far away. Well, I soon found myself thinking about my notes and wondering if the search for happiness through understanding and knowledge couldn't be plotted out on a three dimensional curve with an axis corresponding to each of the variables. I decided that everyone was on this curve with potential for getting up to the top and that if they got to the top they would find Jesus, Buddha, Muhammad and all the others in the history of the world who'd made it to the top. Then it became obvious to me that there had to be many curves because there are many kinds of knowledge and that there would have to be a composite curve to accommodate this. I also realized that people could go up the curve and achieve a degree of understanding, knowledge and happiness that they would forget as soon as they let up on their pursuit of perfection and began to slip back down the curve.

"As you can see, things began to get complicated to say the least. I left the party excited about my thoughts and determined to talk to my friends about them. As Billy might have mentioned, I spent a wild several weeks enthusiastically expounding 'The Curves' to just about anyone who would listen and drinking heavily as I went along. I'm lucky I didn't loose some clients because everyone was sympathetic and seemed to listen, but I'm not sure anyone was hearing, and some of them, I'm sure, thought I'd run off the track for a while, especially when my speech and thoughts got garbled in drink toward the end of our naive, fledgling, philosophical discussions.

"Toward the end, as I tried to explain more and more, the system got hopelessly complicated and evasive. Also I sensed I was becoming somewhat of a bore, and gradually I stopped talking about 'The Curves' except to make slightly joking reference to them at times. I think you could say I started to slip back down my own curve to a pretty low point which is where I am today." With this, Charley had shrugged again and fell silent.

Dr. Shaw had given him a serious look and said, "I wouldn't sell yourself and your curves short, Charley. Your system may not have been perfect, but I don't know of any system that is. I don't think your curves are all that far off the mark, and they may well be the basis for you to step off in new directions that will make your life more meaningful and fulfilled. Beyond a doubt you were playing with the possibility of a higher power at the top of the curve. That's something that should give you hope in your struggle to work through the need for a higher power in the Twelve Step Program."

Still thinking about his unexpected exchange with Dr. Shaw, Charley gave an inward smile of satisfaction as he hit the cue ball toward the triangle of balls at the other end of the table. He was pleased to see three balls scoot into pockets. As he looked around for his next shot, he paused and thought about some of the things the voice had said about action. He wondered more and more about it. If it was to be done without desire then, to be ridiculous, his best shot, at the pool ball he was hoping to knock into the left side pocket, should be aimed without a care in the world whether it went in or didn't.

Come what may! Let God do it! All kidding aside, not wanting to win, to be liked, to be loved, that's a big order. Maybe it's for a saint, but I don't think it's for me, thought Charley.

Come to think of it, that old wizard of a voice talks like he could be Jesus Christ himself. Among other things it's left me more than a little confused about how to act and how not to act. It's un-American not to play to win. That's just about our whole way of life. What's that voice doing around here in my head anyway? Could be it's playing tricks on me. Or am I playing tricks on myself?

The ancient voice seemed to hear Charley complaining about his confusion because it again began to speak:

> O Charley! Many lives of mine as well as of yours have gone by. I know them all, but you do not.
> I am birthless and the Lord of creatures and my Self never changes; yet controlling my own nature, I incarnate myself by my power.
> Whenever religion becomes tarnished and irreligion prevails, I create myself.

My God! Charley thought. There he goes again, all sorts of lives, birthless, changeless, and this time he must be talking about creating divine incarnations: Christ and Buddha and Muhammad and some of those Eastern gods I can't remember the names of. He created them? Excuse me, I'll just have to pass on that one. Talk about thinking big! No question about it though, religion is badly tarnished these days, and so am I, no doubt about that either. I guess I'm ready for a second coming myself. Well, let's get on with it.

The voice started again:

> Actions do not touch me, nor do I desire their results. He who knows me thus is not affected by action.
> Even the wise are confounded about what is action and what is inaction. Therefore I will tell you what is action, knowing which you will be free from evil.

A Game of Chance

That old magician promises everything but the kitchen sink, envisioned Charley. On the other hand, Step Three at the meetings pretty much promises the same thing if you turn your will and life over to the care of God as you understand him, which unfortunately I'm unable to do, lacking a god, among other things. Well anyway let's hear about how to be free from evil; that is if, number one, it can mean free from addictions and guilt. The other evils will have to wait as far as I'm concerned.

The voice resumed its instructions on how to act:

> One has to understand what is action and what is inaction, for the meaning of action is inscrutable.
> He who sees inaction in action, and action in inaction, is intelligent among men.
> Giving up attachment to the fruits of action, being always content, and having no recourse, the wise man does not do anything at all though he becomes engaged in action.
> He who is satisfied with whatever comes by chance, who is unaffected by the dualities of sense contacts, who is without enmity and the same in success or failure does not become bound though he engages in action.

Now he's talking like a gambler, Charley interjected. Is he telling me to take my chances with whatever comes and let it go at that? Win or lose, no difference, everything will be OK! The clinker is you have to do it without desire, love or hate. That's a pretty big order. Maybe I could try it on little things and work my way up. "Out of little acorns grow big trees," Aunt Nellie used to say when she patted my head years ago.

Seemingly without pause, the voice said:

> All work done as sacrifice by the person who is without attachment, who is without egotism, whose mind is established in Self, becomes entirely dissolved.

He who has the understanding that all actions, objects and instruments of action are the Self, realizes the Self, the ineffable Reality.

So he's saying anything and everything is God, reasoned Charley. Realize that, and you'll be free. Take my work and everything else, God, it's yours anyway! That seems to be the message. Well for one thing, God can have my addictions. Just like I think it says in Step Six, I'm ready to have God remove all my defects of character, especially my goddamn addictions. Take them away, God. Please take them away! I hope I'm getting some of this straight, Charley worried. He's coming from an old, old, far-off place, and sometimes his language is queer and hard to guess at, especially when my head isn't all that clear in the first place.

Paying no attention to Charley's criticism, the voice resumed it's way like a bull-dozer clearing out the brush in Charley's head:

Know that through humble submission, repeated inquiry and service, the wise knowers of Truth will instruct you on wisdom.
Even if you are the worst sinner among all the sinners, you will cross over this ocean by the boat of wisdom alone.
As lighted fire turns wood to ashes, so also the fire of wisdom reduces all actions to ashes.

Ashes to ashes, dust to dust. That's it, thought Charley. I'll just burn up the past and be done with it. I don't know that I've been the worst sinner on record, but I must be somewhere in the upper quarter on the list. Can I start over again? "One day at a time," as the AAs and NAs keep on harping at the meetings. I have to start somewhere, sometime. It might as well be today. Also the voice seems to say there's hope after all. It mentions humble submission, which reminds me of Step Seven: Humbly asked Him to remove our shortcomings. And then it says someone will instruct me on wisdom. Who will it be? Where? When? It'd better be soon, or I may not be around to listen.

I don't even have a sponsor, much less a teacher, especially one I could accept. Just yesterday one of the "saved ones" in NA cornered me after the meeting, forced eye-contact and said with intense fervor, "Are you ready to accept Jesus Christ our Lord and Saviour? Pray with me and let him fill your heart with light, love and forgiveness." I had to back off because I didn't want to dampen his enthusiasm, as if anyone could. I remember I said, "Man, I don't disbelieve in him, but that's a personal matter that I don't discuss. Thanks but I don't want to talk about it." Christ! He was aggressive. Said he'd been saved a year ago and wanted to save me. Made me feel very uncomfortable. You can't force a god down someone's throat like that. You'd think they'd learn.

With no comment on that, the voice went on:

> There is nothing so pure here on earth as wisdom. The one perfected by the path of action knows it in himself in the course of time.
> Actions do not create bondage for one who has renounced action through detachment, whose doubts have been sundered by wisdom and who is established in the Self.
> So, O Brave Charley! cut asunder this doubt in your heart born of ignorance with the sword of wisdom. Have faith in wisdom and arise.[3]

Charley stood at the pool table, his cue poised for his shot to put the number three ball in the left side pocket, while all these many words flashed by in his head as if on some fantastic tape or computer screen. That voice is sounding more and more like the Lord of the universe thought Charley. One minute I think I get the gist of it, the next I'm not sure.

I liked what it said about even if I'm the worst sinner among all the sinners I can still make it home to peace and freedom. At least I think that's what it meant. And it said I'd need faith. That's a tall order. You need that for Step Two in the program: Came to believe that a power greater than ourselves could restore us to sanity. That's giving me a lot of trouble. Faith is something I don't have right now. But who knows, it may come, a little at a time. Then too, I think it said if I keep listening and asking someone will come to instruct me about wisdom. Maybe that's what's happening. Far-fetched? Way out? Sure is! But it's better than walking around in a stupid, hopeless vacuum.

Without giving it another thought, Charley hit the cue ball which hit the number three ball which banked against the right side and glided smoothly on the green felt across the table into the left side pocket. Not bad, thought Charley, not bad at all.

CHAPTER SIX

Another Voice Is Heard

Charley was still thinking about that mysterious old voice, wondering if it was just floating about out there in the airwaves waiting to be picked up by anyone who tuned in, or whether it was created specially for himself. No matter, he'd be glad to share it or possibly even be glad to give it away if it got too loud and preachy like some of the "born agains." He'd heard of people speaking in tongues, but he wasn't speaking, he was hearing, and he sure wasn't telling anyone about it.

Charley took a sip of coffee, lit an old-fashioned cancer-causing Camel and started walking slowly down the big wide marble corridor toward the lecture room, cup of coffee in one hand, cigarette in the other. Two more addictions, he mused. They went together, hand in hand. He hated smoking. Two, sometimes three packs a day: cruddy taste, tar-stained teeth, yellowed fingers, foul-smelling odor on his clothes. But he couldn't give it up. He'd tried dozens of times. Heard the nicotine habit was worse than cocaine or even heroin to kick. He could believe it. Well he'd lick it one of these days, as soon as he could. The caffeine could wait. That was easier.

Come to think of it, coffee, nicotine, alcohol and cocaine added up to four addictions. Wonder if they ever thought of developing a Twelve Step Program for quadruple addictions? On the other hand, what would AA and NA do without coffee and cigarettes? They were almost as much a part of the meetings as the Twelve Steps. Oh shit! Enough of this nonsense. One addiction at a time, or at the most two, is plenty to fight, he concluded, as he wandered into the small but comfortable room and slumped into a seat among his now familiar peers in the rehab program.

There was an air of expectancy and curiosity in the room. A small, lean, strikingly handsome man of light tan skin color who appeared to be of East Indian descent was seated in front of the room with Dr. Robert Miller who impressed Charley as being one of the less stuffy, more imaginative and interesting of the staff psychiatrists.

Dr. Miller stood up and began to address the sprawling group of drug addicts and alcoholics.

"We have something new and special for you today, an experiment that I hope will be of help to you as you try to work your way through the difficult and crucial early steps at AA and NA meetings. In particular, I know that many of you have a terribly tough time of it getting past Step Two where a power greater than ourselves is a prerequisite to getting on to the steps that follow. And even if you try to by-pass Step Two for the time being, you find yourselves faced with Step Three where you must turn your will and your lives over to this elusive higher power as you understand him or her or whatever it may be. Today's lecturer may give you some fresh insight into these problems from probably the oldest and certainly one of the most respected philosophical systems in the world.

"I met Keshab Bharati, sitting here beside me, many years ago when I was an undergraduate at Columbia University in New York City. He was teaching a course in Indian philosophy which I attended. I was fascinated by the various Indian yogas or systems he described which seemed to cover all aspects of life, physical and mental, and began a series of personal exchanges and talks with Mr. Bharati that at this point in time have extended well over the last twenty years.

"In recent years, as I became more and more involved in treating patients addicted to alcohol and narcotics, and aware of the life-sustaining support offered them by the Twelve Step Program of Alcoholics Anonymous and Narcotics Anonymous, I have been amazed time and time again to see the similarity between the practical instructions of the Indian yogas, particularly karma yoga, and the essential instructions of Steps Two, Three and Eleven. These steps require a belief in a higher power, turning our will and lives over to that power, and seeking through various ways to improve our contact with that power. They are requirements for recovery which all the rest of the steps use as a foundation.

"It is almost beyond belief to think how wise men in different parts of the world and in different ages have often reached similar conclusions without ever being in touch with each other, although I suspect Mr. Bharati, not to mention the famous psychiatrist C. G. Jung, might say this is too much for pure coincidence.

"Mr. Bharati's subject for today's talk is the Bhagavad Gita. This great book is the most marvelous source of instruction on how to practice karma yoga and, with the exception of hatha yoga, which is the well-known system of physical exercises, the various other yogas of Indian philosophy. For this reason, I have asked Mr. Bharati to give you an introduction to it today, keeping in mind how this unusual little book might help you on your road to recovery.

"Since Mr. Bharati is not one inclined to talk about himself, I'd like to say a few words about his background before he begins. Mr. Bharati comes originally from what used to be called Bengal in India where he studied yoga under the guidance of disciples of Ramakrishna, held by many to be the greatest spiritual figure in recent world history. In teaching in the West, Mr. Bharati has followed in the tradition of Swami Vivekananda, Ramakrishna's foremost and most famous disciple, who aroused great interest in America in the 1890s with yoga concepts attuned to our way of life and our scientific turn of mind. It is Vivekananda who is generally credited with introducing yoga to the twentieth century in the West.

"As part of his classic training, Mr. Bharati spent ten years of pilgrimage, study and meditation in the Himalayas. He is past President of the Ramakrishna Mission College in Calcutta and former editor of *Prabuddha Bharata* (Awakened India), the oldest English philosophical and religious monthly in India today. In the past twenty years, Mr. Bharati has taught yoga and Vedanta philosophy at Columbia and has lectured at Yale, Harvard and other universities. His books, articles, recordings and interviews on radio and television have pioneered and contributed to the current popularity of yoga in the West.

"Enough said, here is Mr. Bharati."

Charley thought the interesting-looking Indian could be anywhere from 35-50 years of age, judging from his appearance and lithe manner as he stood and prepared to talk to his captive audience of old and young, black, white and yellow, male and female addicts in various states and stages of stress, suffering and recovery. But then again, thought Charley, he could be much older. He'd seen some very old men looking very, very young when he'd visited some Buddhist temples during rest and recuperation in Vietnam.

Without hesitation, notes or nervousness, Keshab Bharati began to talk in a voice that if you listened to it long enough had a gentle, hypnotic, yet energizing effect.

"Good afternoon to you recovering people. In India, we have a saying that hemp smokers like to stick together, so the same should apply to ex-hemp smokers looking for help and support.

"I'd like to begin with a quotation from Ramakrishna whom Dr. Miller mentioned as he introduced me. It is from *The Gospel of Sri Ramakrishna* which was edited some years ago with the help of the late Joseph Campbell who afterwards became famous for his writings and series of television programs on mythology. In preparing for today's talk, with Dr. Miller's help, I've learned something of the Twelve Steps and the slogans that are used with them, and this quotation pertains to the "Let God do it" concept expressed in Step Three: Made a decision to turn our will and our lives over to the care of God, as we understood him; and again in Step Eleven: Sought through prayer and meditation to improve our conscious contact with God as we understood Him, praying only for knowledge of His will for us and the power to carry that out. Ramakrishna, who was uneducated and spoke in the style of a simple villager said:

> When the heart becomes pure through the practice of spiritual discipline, then one rightly feels that God alone

is the Doer. He alone has become mind, life and
intelligence. We are only His instruments.
All doubts disappear after the realization of God. Then
the devotee meets the favorable wind. He becomes free
from worry. He is like the boatman who, when the
favorable wind blows, unfurls the sail, holds the rudder
lightly, and enjoys a smoke.

"Well," continued Mr. Bharati, "all of us hope to meet a favorable wind and become free from worry. This is often called the grace of god. I can't quite promise any of you that, but there's always hope, and as Bob Miller suggested, you might find help and support for your work on the Twelve Steps in the Bhagavad Gita. So let me tell you something about it."

Charley, who had been following today's proceedings with more interest than usual thought, favorable wind, my ass! As he says, that's the old God doing it again. Let God do it, let the wind do it, same thing. They really come at you from all directions, north, east, south, west — and wherever that ancient voice comes from, probably another world. Nice homey way of putting it, though. Guess I'll listen for a change and see what this guy has to say. Wonder if he's one of those great gurus you hear about. I suspect Ramakrishna and Vivekananda were, but they must be long since gone.

Mr. Bharati began to talk about his topic of the day:

"The Gita means a song and Bhagavad Gita means the divine song. It is a small book of seven hundred verses and forms part of the vast and ancient Indian epic, the *Mahabharata*, which has a hundred thousand verses in its present form.

"There are uncertainties concerning historical facts dating back at least thirty-five hundred years ago about the Mahabharata and the Gita. One thing, nevertheless, is beyond dispute. The truth of a scripture or of science does not depend on historical facts, though it is true, as Ramakrishna said, that scriptures generally are a mix of sugar and sand, and that one has to separate sugar carefully from sand.

"The Gita belongs to the tradition according to which religion is Truth, a higher truth than science or common experience. It is knowledge not open to the methods of science. It is knowledge more important than the practical knowledge with which we grow food, cook meals, build houses, drive cars, etc. It is knowledge of life's goals, its ideals and the proper way of living. And it is knowledge which is not accessible to sense-observation or intellectual, speculative effort, but without which civilized life disintegrates into the chaos from which it slowly arose, a chaos of which some of you may have had a glimpse.

"The Gita is a sermon on the battlefield. It was delivered by Krishna, the Divine Teacher, to Arjuna, his disciple, on the eve of a great battle between two opposing sets of cousins in which were engaged most of the princes and noblemen of India of the time.

"Arjuna was the leader on one side. He and his brothers were the Pandavas or sons of Pandu. On the other side were Duryodhana and his brothers who were the Kauravas. Both sides were descendants from their common ancestor Kuru.

"Krishna was Arjuna's friend and charioteer. Like Jesus in the West, he is venerated as a Divine Incarnation by the Hindus. His life and character have been delineated in such a manner in the epic and in other historical and religious books that he has become a most endearing idol, the darling hero of the Hindus.

"When Arjuna's chariot was drawn up in front of the opposing army, Arjuna was grief-stricken at the sight of his friends and relatives whom he would have to fight. He was also morally perplexed about his duty as a warrior loyal to king and country because it involved killing his teachers, relatives and friends for the sake of winning kingdoms and wealth. Dismayed and despondent, he sank down in his chariot, reluctant to fight.

"It was at this point in chapter 2, verse 3, that Krishna addressed him with a most stirring call:

> Do not give way to unmanliness, O Son of Partha (Arjuna)! It does not befit you. Discard this petty weakness of heart and arise, O Destroyer of Enemies!

"This is the key appeal of the Gita, to the innate strength and greatness in man."

Charley was sitting bolt upright, eyes wide open. He could hardly restrain himself. Talk about coincidences! This one's outrageous! His nightmare a couple of nights ago was like the horrible situation what's his name, Arjuna, was in, friend and family killing friend and family. Pay no attention to it, he thought, trying to put his amazement aside. Time and time again he'd heard recovering addicts in meetings ascribing everyday coincidences and happenings to their higher power. They'd say asinine things like, "My Higher Power was really with me yesterday. No sooner than I knew I had to talk to my AA sponsor than, bingo! the telephone rang and there he was ready to help." Usually it was perfectly ridiculous and better left unsaid.

Unaware of Charley's excitement and consternation, Mr. Bharati concluded his short introduction to the Gita, saying, "Thus began Krishna's sermon and the message of the Gita which continues on chapter after chapter describing and weaving together various spiritual disciplines that are called yogas.

"The Gita classifies the different ways of knowing God into four broad paths. First, jnana yoga, the way of wisdom; second, bhakti yoga, the way of love of God; third, karma yoga, the way of selfless action; and fourth, dhyana yoga or the way of meditation. These distinctions are not absolute. In practice they are all combined in different degrees by spiritual seekers according to their individual natures. For example, it is not possible to practice karma yoga (or the yoga of action) without practicing some yoga of love and some yoga of wisdom. Again, these are often combined and supported with some daily practice of meditation.

"Though the Gita recognizes many ways of worshipping God, its emphasis, which is also the foundation upon which the Twelve Step Program rests, is on the path of action based on devotion to God who can be both Personal and Impersonal.

"The Gita emphasizes the path of action because religion is not only a personal venture, but a social obligation, which is very much reflected in Step Twelve: We tried to carry this message to alcoholics (and other addicts), and to practice these principles in all our affairs.

"Ramakrishna told his disciples to do whatever they like with the knowledge of one God, both Personal and Impersonal, in their pockets. Krishna makes a similar statement at the end of the Gita in chapter 18, verse 63, when he tells Arjuna:

> This is the wisdom which is more secret than the secret that has been spoken by me. Pondering over it thoroughly, do as you like.

This advice is not a license for wild action, but for the worship of the Divine present in everything.

"Before going further into our exploration of karma yoga and the paradoxes it presents when we try to turn our will and lives over to the care of God, let's pause for a few minutes to talk about that mysterious higher power that's called for in Step Two and which many of you, I understand, find elusive and difficult to believe in. Dr. Miller tells me that the search for a higher power can be so frustrating and hopeless that one patient in desperation declared his higher power to be Mickey Mouse! Well, the Gita says you can have any higher power you want, but that the rewards you get from that power vary with the power's quality. In other words, as they say in this country, you get what you pay for, so that in the case of Mickey Mouse, you might well get a cartoon of Reality instead of the real thing.

"The Divine Incarnation, or Personal God, is the most accessible higher power available to mankind, although needless to say, Divine Incarnation is a mystery.

"Krishna, who is a Divine Incarnation in the Gita, tells Arjuna in chapter 4, verses 6 and 7:

> Though I am birthless and Lord of creatures, and my Self never changes, yet controlling my own nature I incarnate myself by my power.
> Whenever religion becomes tarnished and irreligion prevails, I create myself.

Charley had been following right along, word for word, oblivious of his usual habit, since sitting in organic chemistry classes in long gone college days, of dozing off uncontrollably during lectures. He felt a vague wave of recollection as Mr. Bharati quoted the verses from the Gita about Divine Incarnations. That sounds kind of familiar, he thought. Was it something his friendly old voice had said a few days back? Or was he just imagining it? Shit! His memory wasn't always that good in these days of shattering withdrawal. It didn't really matter. Nothing new about Divine Incarnations anyway. Krishna, the one this smooth-talking Indian is quoting was around thirty-five hundred years ago, but I'll bet no one's seen one lately. Sure could use a DI around this place. Wonder if the second coming is finally on it's way. Charley's mind rambled and wandered on a little as Mr. Bharati lectured on about the quotation he'd given.

"The Power, the Personality that governs the universe, the Power that is All in All, reveals itself in the world around us in time of need in human form. The limited form of a Divine Incarnation such as Krishna, Buddha, Christ—and more recently some would add Ramakrishna—is in nature and obeys its laws ostensibly. However, within these God-like beings there is consciousness of the Supreme Personality who can bestow freedom on others by a glance, by a touch, by its will.

"There is need for authority in every department of life. Management and managers who have the expertise are essential in running the various businesses of society. But the most important business of all is the business of living. We need authoritative utterance from one through whom Truth shines in its utter simplicity and purity.

"Ramakrishna gave a graphic example: suppose you are enclosed in a small place with walls all around. You see only what is inside. But if there is a hole in the wall, you will catch a glimpse of the infinite world beyond. A Divine Incarnation is like that hole through which one catches a glimpse of infinity.

"Ramakrishna also declared that God had made different religions for different people. The various religions are different ways of reaching the one common goal and are suited to the development of worshippers of different kinds. A mother, he indicated, makes strained spinach for her baby, but she cooks rare steak for the grown-ups. The different religions of various higher powers are different creeds or ways, suiting the needs of different worshippers. This is perfectly reflected in the phrase at the end of Step Three: Made a decision to turn our will and our lives over to the care of God, *as we understood Him.*

"Now let's turn our attention to the first part of Step Three: Made a decision to turn our will and our lives over to the care of God. This principle from the gifted founders of AA is the essence of the path of action, or karma yoga, which is the principal theme of the Bhagavad Gita.

"If we turn our will and our lives over to the care of God, then we expect God to take care of us; hence the slogan "Let God do it." This leads us to the conclusion that God is acting through us, which in turn leads to all sorts of perplexities. Here is what Krishna tells Arjuna about this in chapter 4, verses 16-20:

> Even the wise are confounded about what is action and what is inaction. Therefore I will tell you what is action, knowing which you will be free from evil.

One has to understand what is action and what is non-action, for the meaning of action is inscrutable.
He who sees inaction in action, and action in inaction, is intelligent among men.
He whose undertakings are all free from desire and whose sense of being the doer has been burnt by the fire of knowledge, being always content, and having no recourse, he does not do anything at all though he becomes engaged in action.

"In these verses, we hear that man's action is originated by God, the Inner Controller. The wise man, the one who is 'intelligent among men,' knows that Spirit, or Self, is above nature and that God alone acts. He is aware that the action does not belong to him, even though he acts with love or in the spirit of service.

"In Verses 8 through 10 of chapter 5, Krishna becomes more specific:

The man who is united with the Divine knows that in seeing, hearing, touching, smelling, eating, going, sleeping, breathing, speaking, emitting, grasping, and opening and closing eyes, it is his senses which are occupied with their own sensations. He knows that he is doing nothing.
Attributing all action to the Divine, he who works without attachment is not touched by sin, even as a lotus leaf is untouched by water.

"The gist of this is that all activity belongs to nature, and since God creates nature, the ego is very much mistaken when it thinks it is acting. We have to use our imagination, because we are so used to thinking that it is we who act. Imagination is the door to realization. When an idea comes down from head to heart, from imagination to feeling, it becomes real. Reality or Truth is in the hearts of all, beyond all dualities."

Charley was still following along although the going was

getting a little rough and intangible. He was more and more convinced that the verses Mr. Bharati was quoting were out of the same bag of tricks that the voice was using, but the repetition, if it was that, helped. Moreover, Mr. Bharati's comments only served to whet Charley's appetite for more. For the first time in who knows how long, Charley found himself really interested in something that was being said. He sat up straight, took a deep breath and listened as Mr. Bharati continued talking about action.

"Karma yoga, or the path of action, is the dominant theme of the Gita. It is the ideal of service to humanity combined with wisdom and devotion to the Supreme Consciousness. Verses 47 and 48 in chapter 2 give man's ideal of action, which is the ideal of living:

> You have the right to action alone, never to its results. Do not desire results of action nor be attached to non-action.
> Being established in yoga and being the same in success and failure, work without attachment, for evenness of mind is called yoga.

"One who practices karma yoga acts in the world with the idea of service and not with the desire for personal gain. He is neither elated nor disheartened by results. Work is done in the spirit of worship. Such work purifies the mind; Truth is reflected in the purified mind. As the Gita points out in one of the verses I quoted earlier, none can remain absolutely inactive.

"The ideal of self-less action is the goal of man. Action with selfish desire perpetuates the miserable condition of bondage. There are few morsels of pleasure in this world and much misery—as so many of you are very much aware of from your own recent personal disasters. Our hearts remain empty, and we have to turn inward to find fulfillment, the ultimate togetherness that all of us seek.

"Through karma yoga, as through the Twelve Step Program, there is a way out for all. One does not have to retire from the world. One can erode the ego or little self which obscures the Supreme Self or Reality by doing the kind of work one is doing, but in a different spirit. That is why Krishna says karma yoga is skill in action.

"Tolstoy, who in his later years, I think became the world's first hippie, came upon the secret of karma yoga because of his love of truth and compassion. He wrote, 'The work you do out of love without a thought of reward is the work of God.' In the Gita, Krishna urges Arjuna to work like him; that is, like God, without a selfish motive and for the good of all.

"There is some love everywhere, love that is disinterested. A mother works for love of the child. When one works with the idea of service in the spirit of worship without asking any reward, one works like God. True, only a free man can work in that spirit, but a spiritual seeker must begin. In time, the ideas of me and mine, the cause of our bondage, vanish and the Truth manifests itself. Karma yoga begins at home, charity begins at home."

Mr. Bharati paused and looked at his watch, then looked questioningly at Dr. Miller who nodded and smiled. "I think that's about as much as I should try to pack into your heads this afternoon," he said. "I hope I haven't been too much of an egghead talking to you. Some of my best friends are recovering alcoholics, and they tell me that you'll find the most interesting and intelligent people in town at AA meetings. I believe them, so I have made no effort to oversimplify my remarks, as I'm sure you're more than capable of working through them if they strike a chord of promise.

"If you want to know more about the Gita, Dr. Miller can give you the names of one or two translations that are fairly reliable. I have just finished a translation of my own and used my word processor to print out a few copies of chapter 3 which is on karma yoga along with my commentary on the verses.

They'll be here for any of you who might be interested after the lecture.

"Dr. Miller suggested that I leave time for a few questions, so if there are some, I'll be glad to try to give answers."

Interrupting with a sheepish grin, Dr. Miller stood up and said, "Let me start things off, Keshab, if you don't mind, with a question that some of your listeners may be wondering about: Krishna appears as God in the Gita. Can you explain the concept of God that the Gita seems to present?"

Mr. Bharati smiled in return and thought for a few seconds. Then he began:

"God is an English word which means different things to different people according to their moral and intellectual developments. A child understands God in one way, a grown-up person in another, a spiritual person in still another way and finally the saint or the enlightened person knows what God is.

"God is the Self of all. The Gita points out that God is the friend in the hearts of all; he dwells in the hearts of all, making them move like puppets mounted on a machine.

"God is wisdom, says the Gita. God is the origin and God is also the creation. God is the substance of everything; his powers or emanations are the world around us.

"As Gandhi said, 'God is Truth, He alone is, we are nothing.'

"The word for Reality in the Gita is Brahman, which is Pure Consciousness, which is Truth, Love, Purity, Wisdom. There are a thousand names for that Reality. They are all indicators.

"Brahman is both impersonal consciousness as well as the Power which creates the universe. The universe is an emanation.

"God alone exists, there are no other persons. Egos are illusions. The aim of the person who suffers from karma is to realize that his bondage, namely, the sense of the ego, or isolated personality, is a bad dream. Freedom is bodhi or wisdom. Bodhi means enlightenment. It is the substance of all.

"The Gita teaches this Truth. There is no dogmatic idea of the so-called theism or theistic God. Religion is going back to absolute simplicity beyond language and imagination.

"God or no God, Reality is our goal. There is no harm in calling Reality God, for the Inner Ruler in our heart will make it known to us that Truth is within us, that we are Truth.

"It is useless to fight over words. It is like beating down a strawman we have created.

"Our modern world of science and general education needs a higher understanding of man and his true goal amid the conflicting claims of worldliness and Love, which is God who is inside us. The Gita conveys this eternal truth of history."

Mr. Bharati stopped and cleared his throat. Then he said somewhat apologetically, "Well, I got a little carried away with that answer, but it's the way I am, my nature, and I love my subject. If some of you have questions, I promise to be shorter."

A stylishly dressed, handsome woman in her early forties with her right arm broken and in a cast from a drunken fall that had hastened her re-entry (third time around) into the rehab unit raised her good left arm and waved it furiously at Mr. Bharati. He smiled gently and gave her a nod. "I'm having a perfectly awful time finding and accepting a higher power," she said. "Does the Gita say anything that might give me a hint of what to look for?" she asked.

"Let me think," said Mr. Bharati. "There are several places in the Gita that describe the Supreme Spirit. One that comes immediately to mind is in chapter 13, verses 12 through 17, where Krishna says to Arjuna:

> I will now tell you that which is to be known, knowing which one attains immortality. It is the Supreme Spirit without beginning, which is said to be neither existent nor non-existent.
> With hands and feet everywhere, with eyes, head and mouth everywhere, with ears everywhere, it exists

covering everything in the universe.
It is expressed through the actions of all the organs but is without any organ. It is non-attached yet it supports all. It is free of nature, yet it is in it.
It dwells within and without all beings. It is moving and unmoving. It is incomprehensible because of subtlety. It is far and also it is near.
Indivisible it exists as if it were divided in beings. It is to be known as the protector, the end and origin of all beings.
It is the light even of all the lights and is said to be beyond darkness. It dwells in the hearts of all as knowledge, as that to be known and as the Known.

Mr. Bharati had recited the verses so beautifully and with such vibrant conviction, that his audience broke into spontaneous applause, causing one lapsed young man who had drifted off to slip off his chair onto the floor with a loud, crashing thud.

"Are you all right?" asked the concerned lecturer. The young man gave a sheepish grin and waved Mr. Bharati on. He asked, "Another question?"

An older man with white hair and pink face who looked as though he might have spent some time on the pulpit as well as at the bar spoke up, "Is there such a thing as free will in the Gita, or is every action predestined. In other words does the Gita believe in free will or predestination?"

"A good, age-old question, sir," Mr. Bharati acknowledged. "The theological doctrines of predestination and individual freedom create insoluble problems. The Gita proclaims on the basis of the ultimate realization that there is only one person who is the Ruler of all nature. The many and different individuals are not real but apparent existents. The Supreme Person is reflected in the many egos and creates the notion of individuality.

"When it comes to the question of individual freedom we come to this predicament. We do not know who is the individual in the body, nor how free he is. How much control does the individual have over the body he claims as his own? How many choices does he have? Are they his? Still we carry on with a cock-sure belief in our own agency, and we are held responsible for what we call our actions.

"In addition, it is obvious that an individual is often able to reject many promptings from within and choose what he considers right. It is also clear that if he yields to temptations they finally get him. He has then no choice but only compulsions. This road of desire is one of very easy gradient; when you follow it for awhile you hardly realize how far you have gone downhill, and one day when you wake up—as I'm sure many of you have experienced—you discover that you are several thousand feet lower than when you began. It is a hard climb back. Freedom is recovered through faith, as in Step Two: Came to believe that a Power greater than ourselves could restore us to sanity.

"Further, when a person uses his unspoiled sense of freedom to reject impulses, he discovers his freedom increases with the discipline of self-control, his taste changes and he appreciates ideas and ideals which now appear to be worth pursuing. An individual's capacity for intelligent choice is developed. Freedom expands with increasing self-control. One appreciates higher values and pursues them.

"The goal of life, of spirituality, of religion is to attain freedom, or realization, by surrendering ego, self-will to God, as Step Three states: Turning our will and our lives over to the care of God. This attainment comes through practice of selflessness in thought and action. It may take a long time; it may not. It depends on the grace of the Lord within.

"In answer to the question, Have we any free will?, Ramakrishna replied, '. . . God alone is the doer. Do your duties in the world as if you were the doer, but knowing all the time that God alone is the Doer and you are the instrument.'[1] In other words, he suggests that you 'Let God do it,' which I understand is a familiar phrase heard in recovery meetings.

Mr. Bharati glanced once again at his watch and said,

"Time for one more short question."

Charley, who had been lying low trying to take everything in, suddenly remembered his nightmare of a night or two ago, and the horrible dilemma that he seemed to share with Arjuna in trying to decide whether to fight or not to fight and being told by the ancient voice, or Krishna in Arjuna's case, that there was no choice except to fight, even if it meant killing relatives and friends. His hand shot up excitedly. Mr. Bharati said, "Yes, by all means, ask away."

"Mr. Bacardi," stammered Charley, as in his excitement his tongue slipped and he named a famous brand of Cuban rum. The alcoholics in the audience tittered a little nervously. Charley flushed, but regained his composure. "Sorry about that," he apologized. "Let me start over." Charley cleared his throat and began again in a serious tone of voice, "Mr. Bharati, if I'm not mistaken, Krishna advises Arjuna to fight a war against his relatives and friends. Does this mean that the Gita advocates violence?"

With perfect poise despite the distracting ripple of amusement, Mr. Bharati answered, "A very good, apt question. This question comes up often among those who really have not thoroughly studied the work. The Gita points out that non-violence, or 'resist not evil', is the highest virtue; however, society needs protection and cannot remain non-violent in the face of aggression. Violence is never an ideal in a civilized society, but at times, it cannot be avoided if society is to be preserved. Even the terrible action of fighting and killing in war—as Krishna advises Arjuna to do—can be performed as selfless service when lawless societies prey upon others out of greed.

"Individuals who have attained perfection, who have good will toward all in them, do not react with violence, and non-violent resistance is the most civilized method of facing evil. The Gita mentions repeatedly that ahimsa, or non-violence, is the highest virtue. Only very brave, developed individuals can practice it and inspire others to do so.

"The Gita makes a more subtle reference to non-violence that can be closely related to Step Nine: Made direct amends to such people wherever possible, except when to do so would injure them or others. In chapter 17, verse 15, the Gita says that 'Speech which does not cause anxiety . . . (is) called austerity of speech.' Commenting on this, Vyasa elaborates that truthful speech instead of hurting any being should be beneficial because if spoken words hurt beings they do not become meritorious acts or virtue, but become vice. Such vicious truths lead to painful consequences; therefore, one should ponder and speak truth which is beneficial to all beings.

"This application of the principle of non-violence which extends to thought as well as words and deeds is the ideal of the yogi, as the Gita points out toward the end.

"Well, that's about it for today," concluded Mr. Keshab Bharati[2] smiling and looking sympathetically at his struggling group of listeners.

"I realize that my answers have not been all black and white, but these matters never are. You've been a wonderful audience, and should any of you want to discuss some of these things in a more personal way, Bob Miller can tell you how to get in touch with me. My thanks to you, and all my best wishes for your recoveries."

Applause came again as Mr. Bharati shook Dr. Miller's hand and they walked arm in arm out of the lecture hall.

CHAPTER SEVEN

Come Delusion, Come Confusion[1]

Charley was pacing nervously around his small but ample room in the rehab center. He was depressed and felt anxious and mad as hell at the crush of always being surrounded by sobbing, clinging, clawing, limping addicts and outwardly friendly, but often remote and impersonal professionals. He felt like crawling up the wall. A copy of Mr. Bharati's chapter on karma yoga lay untouched on his bedside table. The way things were today, he couldn't read the funny papers, much less a philosophical treatise, no matter how interested he had become in the similarity between what he'd heard Mr. Bharati say and what the voice in his head had seemed to say.

Trying to calm himself, Charley sat down, picked up a deck of cards and slowly and carefully dealt out a game of solitaire, or Canfield as his mother used to call it. He'd been keeping track of his imaginary wins and losses since he'd been here. He imagined that every time he dealt out a hand he bought the deck from the hospital for $52, or $1 per card, and that the hospital paid him back $5 for every card he managed to put above the starting seven stacks of cards from aces on up. He allowed himself to go through the deck only once, one card at a time. Thus far he'd played twenty-seven games and owed the hospital, or the house as he sometimes called it, $650.

Can't win 'em all, he thought and suddenly recalled the summer vacation before he'd dropped out of college when he'd been out West playing piano in a rock band at a fancy dude resort way up in the mountains of Nevada. There'd been great highs when everything fell in place and the improvised music took off by itself suddenly catching fire with everyone playing together as if they'd rehearsed what they were doing. Spontaneous combustion! That's what it was like, thought Charley. And then too, there'd been lots of highs from booze and pot when they weren't playing. They'd take a bottle of

Coors and fill it to the top with pure grain alcohol, 200 proof. Whoosh! What a great summer. Great altitude. Great fun for the young.

Once he had been almost flat broke, down to $60 with payday almost two weeks away. Like other times of financial crisis, Charley had just sort of shrugged it off. He'd never really worried or thought much about money. It had always appeared when he needed it, in the form of a scholarship, or a week-end gig with a band. Or when he was younger from numerous jobs in service stations, grocery stores, drug stores, you name it. He hadn't taken money from his family for much of anything since he was ten or eleven. And by the time he left the University of Iowa and went on the road that summer, he'd been self sufficient for a long, long time. So as was usual with him, he'd decided without much thought that he'd go for broke, bet the $60 all or nothing at all. No point in starving to a slow death. He'd hitched a ride around and around down the horseshoe bends into Reno and gone directly to the El Dorado Casino where he put down $52 for a game of solitaire against the house. He'd said to himself, "Come what may! It's up to the gods!" and guess what? Every single stupid card fell into place smooth as magic, and he walked out with $5 for each of the fifty-two cards, a cool $260! Had one of the gods played the cards? Or was he just lucky? Or was there any such thing as luck? Who knows? Who cares?

Charley became aware that his head was hurting more. He was sure it was going to get worse before it got better. He couldn't play out the solitary game he'd started. The cards blurred before his eyes. He slammed them down on the table. He'd sure like to be somewhere else, anywhere else.

Maybe I'll just run off to those beautiful mountains in the West and live in a cave like a holy man, Charley fantasized. Get away from it all. No people staring at me, no addictions, nothing to do but breathe pure, clean air. Read somewhere once that great yogis aren't bothered by heat or cold and can live on air alone, although I think they call it prana, not air. Must be some kind of pure energy, he thought. Wouldn't mind some of that! No hang-overs or hang-ups. Make your own out of thin air. Be a lot better than using alcohol or coke!

Pack up and head for the hills, that's what I should do, his mind soared on with the unhindered, free imagination of a fourteen year old juvenile. But I probably won't go anywhere for a good long time, he almost moaned out loud, plummeting to earth with a thud. Suddenly he got up and pounded his fists rapidly and hard against the solid old wall until they began to bleed. He began to pace nervously again, feeling persecuted and desolate, sucking away at his bleeding knuckles.

In desperation, Charley threw himself wildly down onto the bed, miserable as all get out; he found himself muttering, "Come delusion, come confusion. Come delusion, come confusion." The words seemed to come mysteriously from the deep, forgotten recesses of his mind, the words of a magician casting a spell.

He liked the sound of the words and, like waving a wand, said them over again and again, each time more calmly. Gradually, his breathing became quiet, slower and rhythmical in pace with the words. At last, he closed his eyes and as though a spell had been cast felt a soft, soothing glow come over his being, as words again began to flow in his head from the ancient old voice.

The voice began:

> O Charley! When a person renounces all desires and is not attached to sense objects, he is said to be settled in the path of contemplation.
> Save the mind by the mind. Do not depress the mind. The mind itself is the mind's friend as also its enemy.

Charley thought right on the button, old fellow. Not only is my mind depressed, it's running rampant and wild around in my head, and I'm afraid I'm going to crash again, or slip as they call it around this fucking place. I don't want to crash, it'd only louse things up more than they are already. Would you believe I was almost ready to bash my head in

Come Delusion, Come Confusion

against that wall? Can you help me with wise words from the East, old and ancient friend? Or am I hoping for too much too soon?

Making no promises, the voice continued without pause:

> The mind is a friend of him who has conquered the mind by the mind. The mind itself acts like an enemy for him whose mind has not been subdued.
> The self of one who has conquered his mind and has attained peace is the same in heat and cold, pain and pleasure, honor and dishonor.
> He who is samesighted toward friends, companions, enemies, neutrals, the odious, consorts, saints and sinners is outstanding.

Is he telling me not to get annoyed with anyone in this place, wondered Charley? Treat addicts and psychiatrists and social workers the same? No like, no dislike? If I could only withdraw from them all and still be on the scene, watching it, but safely removed from it, that would be great, or at least I think it might be, cautiously qualified Charley.

The voice had more to say:

> The yogi should always practice concentration of mind alone in a quiet spot, restraining body and mind without desire and without possessions.

Did he hear me thinking that I might just run off to the mountains and live in a cave like a holy man, loin cloth and all, Charley continued to wonder. I think he may be telling me how to get away from it all. I'm not sure I was really serious about that escape route. Not too practical, especially in winter, but I'm willing to listen.

The inscrutable voice went on with its instructions:

> One who wants to practice meditation should place his seat firmly on a clean spot, neither too high nor too

low, and cover it with tender grass, deer skin and cloth, one above the other in that order.
Taking his seat there and making the mind one-pointed by restraining its activities and those of the senses, he should practice meditation for self-purification.
Holding the spine, the neck and the head steadily in a line and gazing at the tip of the nose without looking in any direction and without movement, the yogi of peaceful mind, fearless and established in the vow of celibacy, should sit absorbed in me by controlling his mind.

He's speaking as though he's my Inner-Self again thought Charley. And he's saying that nothing physical should be on the mind, not even sex. That's a tall order, to get rid of sex as well as all my other addictions. I don't think that's a likely possibility. Matter of fact I don't think any of it is possible without some of that fair wind of grace that Ramakrishna, according to Mr. Bharati, said was always blowing. "Blow some my way," to quote that famous old ad headline for Chesterfields, mused Charley recalling trivia from his days in the advertising business. His unsteady mind roved on to the tremendous pressures, long liquid lunches and cocaine filled joys of the high-flying profession that had brought him right to the brink of the disaster he was in now. It hadn't taken much to push him over. Breaking away from this remembrance of things past, his thoughts returned again to the voice. OK old voice, go ahead, "Blow some my way," he thought. I sure could use some help.

Like a soft, gentle breeze, the voice kept on its course through Charley's head:

Thus absorbed in me constantly, the self-controlled yogi attains the supreme peace of Freedom which is my nature.
A lamp in a windless place does not flicker. Know this to be the example of the concentrated mind of the yogi.

> That where the mind stilled by the practice of
> concentration rests, where the self seeing the Self
> delights in the Self;
> And gaining which he does not consider any other gain
> superior, and established in which he is not shaken by
> the severest of pain;
> Know that to be complete absorption of mind in Spirit
> which is complete cessation of painful contacts. This
> should be practiced with fortitude and a mind free from
> attachment.

Wow! That's some state of mind to be in exclaimed Charley to himself. Free from pain, free from all confusion and delusion and full of delight. I'll bet not one person in a billion can concentrate his mind like that in this day and age. Maybe in another time. I'm not sure how up-to-date this hypnotic old voice is, but he sure takes my mind away from the cesspool it's been in today.

Neither encouraged nor discouraged by Charley's insistent interruptions, the voice resumed:

> Drawing the restless and wandering mind away from
> wherever it turns to, the yogi should bring it under the
> control of the Self.
> Supreme happiness comes to this yogi whose mind is
> peaceful, who is without distractions, who is stainless
> and who has become one with the Supreme Self.
> He who has achieved this state is same-sighted
> everywhere and sees the Self in all the beings and all the
> beings in the Self.

Man, oh man! thought Charley. Now he's really talking about the Higher Power of all higher powers. All in everything, all in All. I'm starting to think there might be something in it for me, my own higher power, at least one I could accept without a lot of hocus-pocus. I'll keep thinking about it. You never know what's going to happen, although I'm not sure thinking has much to do with it.

The now familiar ancient one talked on:

> I am never lost to him who sees me everywhere and all in me; nor is he lost to me.
> O Charley! He who sees with an equal eye the pleasure and pain of all, as he sees his own, is regarded as the best yogi.

That's all great thought Charley to himself, but my mind, for one, is restless, turbulent, strong and obstinate. As the old voice might say, I think its control, even if I had no addictions, would be as difficult as that of the wind.

The voice responded to Charley's doubts:

> Doubtless the mind is restless and difficult to control, but it can be restrained, O Charley! through practice of meditation and renunciation of desires.
> Union with the Supreme Self is difficult to achieve, I agree, by one who is not self-controlled, but it is possible for one with self-control through persistent practice of concentration and detachment.

Remembering his many slips and crashes, Charley wasn't sure he could ever find the strength and discipline to practice anything like this for long and wondered what happens to a person who tries hard only to have his mind slip away without succeeding in his practice. Questioning words flowed into his head, catching the poetical manner of the voice:

> O Ancient Voice! What road does a person of faith but of no application travel when his mind slips from these practices without achieving perfection in them?

With understanding and compassion, the voice in Charley's head replied:

> O Charley! Such a person is never lost here or hereafter.

> My Friend! No doer of good ever comes to grief.
> Gaining the worlds where the righteous go and
> dwelling there for many years, the person who has
> slipped from the path of yoga is born in the house
> of the pure and affluent.
> Or he is born in the family of learned yogis. Such a
> birth in the world is rarer.
> There he, O Charley! recollects the last life's under-
> standing of the spiritual aim and struggles evermore
> for perfection.
> Because of past habit, he is drawn helplessly, as it were,
> toward Perfection. Even an inquirer after this Supreme
> Goal reaches beyond the ritualism of religions.

Charley's suspicions were aroused by these promises. They were too good to be true, like some of the others the voice made. If life worked that way, why hadn't anyone told him about it before. Still, this compassionate voice with its learned sentences had to be coming from somewhere. He couldn't be making it up. It was as though it was recorded on a compact disc and played through a receiver in his head. Talk about modern science! Had he been a yogi in his last life, or the one before that? Was it all coming back to him now, when he really needed help to go on with this life? Questions, questions and more questions. And any answers required faith, no proof seemed to exist except that in his head.

The voice kept on:

> Striving harder than before and becoming free from
> stain, he achieves Perfection after many births and
> realizes the Supreme Self.
> The yogi is higher than the ascetic, higher than the
> learned scholar, higher than the worker. Therefore, O
> Charley! become a yogi.
> Among all the yogis, one who worships me with faith
> and with his heart devoted to me is the best in my
> opinion.[2]

Well that's some statement thought Charley, his overwhelming depression and anxiety all but forgotten in the mystical flow of words in his head. I really don't think I'm cut out to live in a cave and meditate forever, but I'd like to try meditation, and if I could slowly and gradually develop some faith in a higher power along with it, who knows, I might be ready to try another stretch outside these cold, historic stone walls.

Strange, how the old voice never seems far from the Twelve Steps. When it was talking about concentration and meditation, it was getting close to Step Eleven: Sought through prayer and meditation to improve our conscious contact with God *as we understood Him*, praying only for knowledge of His will for us and the power to carry that out.

Maybe Mr. Bharati might be willing to teach me how to meditate, Charley speculated. That might be really interesting. Perhaps, if he could only pull himself together and work up his courage, he'd ask Dr. Miller's advice about it next time he saw him around in the halls.

Feeling calmer now, Charley got up from the bed knowing that his capacity for philosophical thought was pretty well exhausted for the moment. Enough is enough, he thought. He looked at the unfinished game of solitaire, sat down and started to play it out. As he began going through the deck one card at a time, all four aces surfaced in the first ten cards. He carefully placed them above the seven neat piles and wondered how his luck was going to run for the rest of the day.

CHAPTER EIGHT

A Mind-bending Trip

Much to his surprise, Charley was in New York City with three of his fellow-inmates from the rehab center. He'd asked Dr. Miller if he thought Mr. Bharati might be willing to tell him how to experiment with meditation, and without hesitation Dr. Miller had said he'd try to set up an appointment if some of the other patients were interested enough to go along and turn the outing into a field trip that would be within the limits of the rehabilitation program prescribed by the hospital. Three others had volunteered for the excursion, and Dr. Miller had set up a 2:00 Saturday afternoon appointment for them with Mr. Bharati at his studio on East 81st Street.

The four of them had caught a train midmorning from Philadelphia that arrived in Grand Central at 11:30. They were a strange, mismatched looking quartet of recovering addicts.

Charley, the Vietnam veteran, retired musician and former advertising account executive, was in his early thirties, handsome, youngish, still looking physically fit, and for a change, freshly dressed and clean shaven.

Patty, the stylishly-dressed woman, with her broken arm in a cast and sling, was an imposing figure in her early forties. She was a newspaper columnist and novelist, brilliant and intelligent. She was successful but probably too sensitive to withstand the brutal competition and rough life of the world of publishing. Her speech usually was slightly slurred by the heavy dose of valium, or who knows what else, her psychiatrist prescribed to keep her circulating in the everyday world, or in this case the rehab center. She tended to smile and look you in the eye after saying something, as though asking for your approval.

The third member of the group was Samson, a bright, intelligent-looking black man with huge bulging muscles in his arms and legs that almost burst through his clothes. He was about Charley's age, 6'4" in height, weighed close to 240 pounds and towered like a coal-black giant over his fellow travelers. He was a stone mason who might have been an artist in stone had he had more training and opportunity. He had fallen onto bad times trying to please and be accepted by the rednecks he worked with on construction jobs. Boiler-makers (a shot of whiskey gulped down all at once followed by a glass of beer) during the lunch break and after work had been too much for him. He liked Jesus and was doing well working away at the Twelve Steps. He had promised Dr. Miller to do his best to keep the group together and out of trouble. New York City was an easy place to slip in. Temptation lurked and leered at you from practically every corner in one form or another.

Of the four "sodden seekers," as they had jokingly referred to themselves on the train, Mary was the least noticeable. She was a mousey, slight little woman in her late twenties, the mother of two small children and wife of an overly ambitious and successful entrepreneur in the plastic molding business. She looked beaten, lacked color and seemed bent over in despair. She hadn't been able to bear the pressures of the unrelenting, insistent demands of motherhood and the harsh, inconsiderate ultimatums of her husband on his way to fame and fortune and all the pleasures of life. Mary had succumbed to an overdose of tranquilizers and vodka. She didn't say much at the rehab center, although today she had managed an occasional weak smile and several yes and no responses to the well meaning attentions of the other three as they wended their way from taxi to train to subway on their trip into the big city.

The four of them were at the Metropolitan Museum of Art, only a block and a half from Mr. Bharati's studio. Charley, who knew the City well, had escorted them down into the Lexington Avenue subway, and they had ridden up to 77th Street, glad to have Samson along to protect them from the threat of muggers, panhandlers and other creatures that inhabited the bowels of the city. Climbing stairs to the street, they had walked up 80th over Park Avenue and past Madison Avenue, admiring the elegant town houses and massive apartment buildings from another era, to Fifth Avenue where they found themselves facing the beautiful, long steps and classic facade of the art museum.

Suddenly, without warning, they were surrounded by a whirling, dancing group of young people dressed in orange robes and tennis shoes. Their complexions seemed pale, and the shaved heads of the young men glistened in the afternoon sun. They thumped tambourines and clashed tiny cymbals together as they danced and sang with great enthusiasm:

Hare Krishna, Hare Krishna, Krishna Krishna, Hare Hare;
Hare Krishna, Hare Krishna, Krishna Krishna, Hare Hare.
Hare Rama, Hare Rama, Rama Rama, Hare Hare;
Hare Rama, Hare Rama, Rama Rama, Hare Hare.

"Do you follow Krishna, Rama or Hari?" asked Charley as he dropped two dollars into a basket held by a slim, clean-shaven young man who was bobbing up and down in rhythm to the boisterous chanting of the others. "All three, or take your pick," half-sang the devotee in perfect rhythm as he and the vibrating troupe bounced on and on down Fifth Avenue toward Central Park.

"Do you suppose they sensed why we're here?" Charley questioned and smiled. "You'll find anything and everything in New York," he continued, as he took Mary by the hand and they all climbed the gradual slope of steps leading into the museum.

With an hour and a half remaining before their date with Mr. Bharati, they decided to lunch in the cafeteria and walked down the long, elegant hall of pink marble, lined with ancient Greek heads and statues, that leads to it. The sculptures were all in muted tones of tan and red. What a great atmosphere thought Charley, momentarily forgetting his problems and loving the sense of beauty and history that surrounded him.

They had simple lunches in the lovely old dining area during which they tried unsuccessfully to avert their eyes from the surrounding tables where many of the patrons were happily drinking beer and wine with their food. Afterwards, they decided to split for forty-five minutes because everyone wanted to see something different in the vast recesses of the museum. Patty wanted to see the new exhibit of French Impressionist paintings; Charley, who had visited several Buddhist temples when he was in Vietnam and was sort of attracted to Asian art, wanted to go to the Oriental galleries; Samson wanted to inspect the huge ancient Egyptian temple that had been rebuilt stone for stone without mortar in a special wing of the museum; and Mary said she thought she'd just sit and rest in the tiny medieval chapel with beautiful stained glass windows they'd passed before finding their way to the cafeteria. They all went off in their own separate directions, promising to meet at the information desk in the flower bedecked Great Hall with at least fifteen minutes to spare before their appointment with Mr. Bharati.

Charley, who'd visited the museum a few times before, caught up with Mary and guided her back to the little chapel, fearing she might not find it and would be too timid to ask for directions. Then he ambled along from room to room, working his way toward one of his favorite spots, where stairs led to the second floor and the displays from the Orient. As he approached the Great Hall, the noise and clamor of visitors grew louder. With relief, he turned to his right and walked into the serene, unexpected quiet of an Italian Renaissance courtyard. A large marble fountain gurgled gently and musically in a corner. Pleasing green plants and trees and numbers of white, mostly male, statuary frolicked around the room. Some of the figures were wearing a modest fig leaf, others not. Such classic beauty and quiet, thought Charley, as he paused to gaze at a black casting of a handsome young Greek boy picking a thorn from his heel. How wonderful it was to be out of the hospital and sober, if only for a day. Even if this afternoon should turn out to be a total, embarrassing flop, just to be here made the

A Mind-bending Trip

trip worthwhile for him. He cast a lingering look around the courtyard, and started up the stairs past the Greek boy to the second floor.

Reaching the top, he looked for a last time from the open balcony at the silent Renaissance scene in the empty court yard below and began to walk in the direction of the Eastern galleries. Along the way, he stopped to admire an exquisite collection of Chinese porcelains in delicate shapes and sizes and fantastic, mesmerizing glazes of cobalt blue, apple green, onyx and purest white. He stared long into the rich ox-blood depths of a small artist's water bowl, and his mind went far away. Could be there's a higher power hiding in those hypnotic depths, he thought as he pulled himself back to the other treasures surrounding him. Maybe that's why people pay so much for art, because there's something mystical and near-perfect about it.

Charley moved on and soon found himself at his destination. He was in a huge room. There were two or three other visitors quietly moving from object to object; otherwise, it was deserted except for about fifteen life-size statues of Buddhist figures. Lots of female Kuan-yins scattered about. Hope these ladies are in good working order today, thought Charley. As I recall, their specialty is mercy or grace, and I sure could use some. I'm still waiting for that fair wind that Ramakrishna talked about.

As he reflected, Charley's attention was drawn to the center of the gallery where a life-size golden Buddha stood in front of a Chinese Buddhist fresco predominantly in beautiful shades of faded red and green. It must have been forty feet long and twenty feet high and well over a thousand years old.

A little awed, Charley sat down on a black leather cushioned bench placed about twenty feet in front of the Buddha. He crossed his legs, relaxed and looked at the scene, absorbed in it. After a few minutes he got up and walked up close to the golden figure. He stared fixedly at the face. The compassionate one stared back and began a series of rapid transformations. It winked at him, closed one eye, closed the other eye, changed form this way and that producing different images, peaceful yet powerful. Charley closed his eyes to stop the fluid-like changes. But as he opened them, the shining Buddha continued his flickering progressions. For a moment, Charley wondered what was going on and drew back from the figure with its upraised hands signifying peace. He covered his face with his hands, and the old intonation of the magician, "Come delusion, come confusion!" passed through his head.

Then, Charley dropped his hands and smiled. He wasn't frightened. He remembered that since the age of fourteen, when he had stared long and hard at a picture of his cousin Emily whom he had a crush on, he had known this kind of harmless hallucination. It happened if he looked at anything intensely enough; even his own face in the mirror would change form after form after form if he stared hard at it. He believed from long experience that this visual hocus-pocus meant nothing, was harmless and should be paid no heed. The unexpected quickness and golden source of the episode had taken him by surprise. That was all that had happened. He wasn't unpleased.

Enough of this, he thought, I've still got the afternoon ahead of me. He looked at his watch. Where had the time gone? It was time to meet the other three in the Great Hall downstairs. He nodded affectionately to the goddesses, cautiously gave a hidden wave of the hand to the mysterious, friendly Buddha and made his way down the majestic main stretch of marble stairs to his rendezvous at the information booth.

The four recovering friends met as planned, with no slips or mishaps, and walked the short distance from the museum to the somewhat run-down town house on 81st Street that housed Mr. Bharati's studio. It was 2:00 PM. They were exactly on time. Charley rang the bell in the entranceway, and a buzzer responded to let them inside to a small foyer that allowed access to the various apartments the house had been divided into. They found themselves facing a carpeted flight of stairs, and Mr. Bharati appeared at the top, smiling and motioning them to join him.

Charley was a little excited, and bounded up the stairs saying, "Hi, I'm Charley," as he shook Mr. Bharati's proffered hand which was smooth, with a firm grip. Funny, thought Charley, at the lecture I thought he was a small man, but today he looks big. More slowly the others came up to be greeted, each giving their first name which was all that was allowed in Twelve Step meetings and at the rehabilitation center.

Mr. Bharati gestured for them to enter his studio, the door to which was open in front of them. As they went in he said, "Please sit down anywhere and make yourselves comfortable." The room was strikingly furnished. An orange sofa caught your eye as you entered. Soft-colored prints of illumined figures in Indian cave paintings hung over it. The floor was covered with a thick green rug, and a ten foot tall screen printed with tiny glittering gold stars hid a small kitchen area. Two sitars were placed on either side of an old marble fireplace. A dancing Shiva was on Mr. Bharati's desk with a photograph of a stone Buddha over it. There was a door leading to a small adjoining bedroom. The main room had a high ceiling painted sky-blue and was big, neat and peaceful. It looked as though it had been freshly vacuumed. The four travelers were relieved to be there. The noise of the city seemed far, far away.

Mr. Bharati said, "I'm delighted to have you here. Dr. Miller said that you had expressed an interest in meditation and thought you might like to know how some of us practice it."

Charley said, "We were all talking on the train, and sort of hoped you would show us a technique that we could practice on our own. Even Samson, who says he has a real live higher power working 'up there' for him, said he'd like to see what it's all about. I guess the rest of us would just like to see if it helps."

"Well," said Mr. Bharati, "let me tell you something about meditation the way I teach it. First, it's a step-wise sequence of instructions designed to calm and quiet the body and mind. This involves sound and breathing as well as thinking. It even takes into account your sense of smell," he said as he reached into the desk and took out a faintly scented stick of amber incense which he lit and placed in a nearby burner.

"When you meditate," he continued, "your spine, neck and head should be in a straight line so that you can sit motionless and comfortable, and not be mindful of the body, throughout the meditation. The best way to do this is to sit crossed-legged on the floor, which I will demonstrate later on. To do this with ease may take some time and practice, so for today you can sit where you are, as straight as you can comfortably manage.

"All these preliminaries are to help free you from the body and to quiet the continuous thought processes that go on in our heads about this and that desire or problem.

"The meditation I'm going to lead you through is based on a series of steps recommended by Vivekananda in *Raja Yoga*, his book on a scientific approach to control of mind and body. As Dr. Miller mentioned the other day, Swami Vivekananda came to this country in the 1890s and was a brilliant, energetic, flamboyant young man who is often credited with laying the groundwork for much of the interest in yoga that has surfaced in recent years.

"As we go through the meditation you'll hear Indian chants that would be impossible for you to duplicate, should they appeal to you. With this in mind, I've taped a similar meditation and have copies for you to take when you leave. You may want to use the tape as an aid to your meditation. Also you should know that terminology relating to your favorite god or ideal, if you have one, can be used as you see fit.

"As to the purpose and goal of meditation, it could be said to be the search for the Supreme Self or Reality, as it is sometimes called.

"The idea of reality is derived from within us from self-consciousness. Reality means substance, a datum which is the same under all circumstances though its qualities may change. There is no such thing in observed nature. Nature is quality, but it is ever in a state of change. The belief in the substantiality of nature is just a practical belief. It is derived from self-

A Mind-bending Trip

consciousness and is superimposed upon fleeting groups of changes or distinctions created by the senses.

"It is only in samadhi or in superconscious experience that we are aware of what substance is; in ordinary experience the substance of pure consciousness is always mixed with and contaminated by changing thoughts, feelings and sensations. When consciousness is absolutely pure, call it pure thought or feeling, without any change obscuring or limiting its steadiness or unlimitedness, then we know what substance, reality or Self is.

"All life, all activity is for the purpose of getting at this elusive substance which we have in language but not in our experience. This is what we seek and search for vainly outside in the time-space universe of change, which is maya, the mystery of creation and our futile effort to find happiness in sensation.

"The search for God and freedom and happiness is the search for substance. Worldliness is the abuse of substance. Ethics and religion are the right conduct for recovering from addiction to the pseudo-substance of the world. The real substance is within; it is the Reality, the Self and the purest delight without any reaction. Worldliness is seeking it outside in glamor and sensation. Drawn outside by the semblance of substance, we run into ruin, but the road to recovery and sanity is always open. The breeze of grace blows for all who have faith and who pray. When we seek substance outside and in sensation, love dies and the heart dries up.

"Well, that's quite a bit to say in one breath, isn't it," said Mr. Bharati, smiling and hoping his words had created a helpful impression in the minds of the four recovering substance abusers.

"Before we begin the meditation, let me quote for you a poem about the goal of meditation by Vivekananda that I translated this morning from the original Bengali for you to hear."

Mr. Bharati produced a scrap of paper from his shirt pocket and began to read to the group:

Swami Vivekananda as a wandering monk

A Mind-bending Trip

There is neither the sun, nor the lovely moon, nor a star.
In the infinite space floats shadow-like the image universe.
In the primeval, undivided mind the world-process floats;
It floats and sinks and rises again in the ceaseless stream of 'I am'.
Slowly the throng of shadows depart and merge in the primal abode.
Now flows unbroken the feeling of pure 'I' and 'I' alone.
That flow also ceases, void merges in the Void.
Beyond the reach of speech and mind.
He knows whose heart knows.

The group of four was held in a spell. Mr. Bharati, poised as ever, silently got up from his swivel chair at the desk and proceeded to sit on the floor facing his visitors. He neatly tucked his left heel under himself and placed his right heel above it with his knees resting comfortably on the floor. He rested his arms on his thighs, palms up. He said, "This is the way you can learn to sit with a little practice. It is called the easy posture because it is so comfortable once your muscles stretch and accommodate to it. If it is too difficult, you can learn to sit comfortably cross-legged, but this is better. Now, if you'll sit as upright and be as comfortable as you can, we'll begin."

Charley and his companions shifted and squirmed this way and that way trying to get in readiness for the meditation. Charley was wondering, what have I let myself in for this time?

Mr. Bharati closed his eyes, sat silently with his eyebrows drawn together in concentration for a short time and then began to chant in melodious rolling tones a Sanskrit poem or hymn. He followed this in English with a salutation to the Supreme Spirit, then told the group that the body is the temple of the spirit, perfect in every part. In sequence he mentioned the various parts and organs of the body as being pure, clean, healthy and strong. Next he softly said to breathe out and then as you breathe in to feel a radiant stream of energy purifying and relaxing the body, as before in every part, part by part. Breathing out, he said to expel impurities, anxieties, fears and superstitions. After this Mr. Bharati said to send thoughts of love and well-being to all those near and dear and to all the beings in the universe, East and West, North and South, above and below. Now, continued Mr. Bharati, pray to all the illumined beings, the shining saints of the past and present, and most of all to our Innermost Self, for light and guidance, wisdom and strength. At this point, he suggested that each person feel that they were a pure witness, observing all their thoughts and actions, but unattached, unaffected, unchanging. Some minutes of silence followed.

Softly again, Mr. Bharati instructed the group to breathe in inwardly repeating Om, the Sanskrit sound symbol for the Supreme Spirit, and this time to feel a current flowing down the spine to its base, striking at the dormant energy lying there. Breathing out, he instructed them to feel the current rising along the spine to the center of the heart, opening up there the center of spiritual truth and understanding; to feel a light touching the heart; to be immersed in this light, dissolving in it. He said to concentrate on this light in the heart area near the spine and commenced with more Sanskrit chanting. He ended in a silence that lasted for several minutes.

The silence was broken gently with more rhythmical Sanskrit chanting. It was a phrase hypnotically repeated over and over and over again, starting out slowly and ending in a whisper of rapid repetitions:

> Om, namo Sri Bhagavate
>   Ramakrishnaya, namo, namo.
> Om, namo Sri Bhagavate
>   Ramakrishnaya, namo, namo.
> Om, namo Sri Bhagavate
>   Ramakrishnaya, namo, namo . . .

A Mind-bending Trip

A deepened state of silence in what seemed to be a charged atmosphere ensued that lasted for a few minutes more. Now Mr. Bharati chanted briefly again and told the group to take a few deep breaths and return to the plane of everyday consciousness feeling refreshed and renewed, healthy and strong, calm and relaxed. With ease Mr. Bharati jumped up and returned to his desk chair. The others remained momentarily transfixed, trying to return to their surroundings.

Mr. Bharati looked at his watch and said, "Unfortunately, I have another appointment in a few minutes, but there is time for some questions, if you'd like."

To everyone's surprise, Mary who seemed to have better color and a spark in her eye, spoke up, "You used Om often in your chants, can you tell us something about it?"

"Certainly," said Mr. Bharati. "You all must have heard of Transcendental Meditation which built up a huge following in the 1970s and still is practiced by many. The basis of T.M. was the repetition of a mantra which they attempted to assign according to a person's nature without knowing much, other than a birth date, about the person.

Om, said Mr. Bharati, drawing out the smooth, engulfing sound, is a universal mantra. You can use repetitions of Om as a mantra in meditation, or actually any time you please. It is the most sacred sound symbol of Divinity and has been used by followers of Sanatana Dharma, the Eternal Religion of the Hindus, from the earliest of times.

"Let me read to you briefly what Vivekananda said about it." Getting up, he extracted a volume from a long line of similar ones in a bookcase on the opposite wall. He found his place and read:

> The idea 'God' is connected with hundreds of words, and each one stands as a symbol for God. Very good. But there must be a generalization among all these words, some substratum, some common ground of all the symbols and that which is the common symbol will

be the best, and will really represent them all. In making a sound we use the larynx and the palate as a sounding board. Is there any material sound of which all other sounds must be manifestations, one which is the most natural sound? Om, spelled Aum, is such a sound, the basis of all sounds. The first letter A is the root sound, the key, pronounced without touching any part of the tongue or palate. M represents the last sound in the series, being pronounced by the closed lips, and the U rolls from the very root to the end of the sounding board of the mouth. Thus Om represents the whole phenomena of sound producing. As such it must be the natural symbol, the matrix of all various sounds. It denotes the whole range and possibility of all the words that can be made . . .
Om has around it all the various significances of Divinity, Personal, Impersonal or Absolute God. As such it is the universal sound symbol of divinity.

Mr. Bharati closed the book with a snap and said with great enthusiasm, "Isn't he wonderful? He brought yoga to this country, he practically saved India, and he didn't live to be forty!"

Samson had been waiting to ask a question. "I've been saved by Jesus." he said. "Is there any connection," he asked, "between Christianity and the type of approach your meditation suggests which I assume is based on Hinduism?"

"There is no conflict and much similarity," answered Mr. Bharati. "Many authorities believe that the origin of Christianity was greatly influenced by Eastern thought.

"The Hindus venerate Christ as an Incarnation, and they see that his essential message is that of the Sanatana Dharma, the Eternal Religion of the Hindus. The special ethical and religious ideas contained in the teachings of Christ have no antecedents in the religious tradition in which he was born. Non-resistance to evil, love of enemies, monastic practices, love of death, the assertion of man's innate perfection (the kingdom of heaven is within you), universalism and the like are principles not to be found in the religion into which he was born.

"Many incidents in Christ's life, the organization of the Catholic Church and its rituals suggest a Buddhistic and Hindu origin. The Gospel stories of the immaculate conception of a virgin mother, the miraculous birth, the story of slaughter of the infants by Herod, and the chief events of Christ's life seem like repetitions of what happened in the lives of Krishna and of Buddha. The idea of incarnation is purely an Indian idea. It was not known among the Jews. The star over Buddha's birthplace and the prophecy of the old monk Asita are repeated in the Gospel story of Simeon. The temptation of Buddha by Mara, the evil spirit, the twelve disciples with the principal disciple Ananda and the many miracles recall the stories in Christ's life. I could go on and on. There are innumerable similarities between Hindu-Buddhist practices and doctrines and those of Christianity."

Mr. Bharati paused and Patty, who had been waiting patiently with a question, broke in to ask, "Mr. Bharati, I thought your meditation was lovely and very effective, but many of us including myself simply do not have the attention span at this point in our lives to practice it by ourselves, even with a tape. I know you talked about karma yoga, the yoga of action, the other day and I can see how some of us can work at that, but I keep wondering if there isn't some easier way to help us with our difficulties in this day and age?"

"Yes, of course, you wonder correctly, and there is an easier way if it suits your nature," commented Mr. Bharati. "It is bhakti yoga, or the yoga of the love of God. This requires faith and devotion, most often to a form or manifestation of God. From the little Mr. Samson has said, I suspect he practices it. Our faith and devotion keep wavering in the beginning of spiritual life, but through persistent effort and doggedness, they become stable and firm by the grace of the Divine. As I indicated in my lecture, Ramakrishna says that a boatman has to steer his boat out of a narrow creek slowly and carefully and sometimes by pulling it with a rope, but once it reaches open waters, he unfurls the sail to the wind and sits in repose at the hull smoking a pipe. Stability in character requires steady and long practice.

"As indicated in Step Three in the Twelve Step Program where we turn our will and our lives over to the care of God, God takes care of all the needs of the devotee who relies on him completely. My teacher, Swami Shivananda who was a disciple of Ramakrishna, wrote in a letter, 'Take the Lord's name without end. Let the heart be filled with His name; you will not in that case feel any kind of want—whether it is material or moral or spiritual. It is only due to lack of faith in the Lord and of devotion and love for Him that the above-mentioned wants are felt.'"[1]

At that moment, the door bell rang. Mr. Bharati jumped up and said, "Please, stay where you are, he is early." He went out the door and perilously down the stairs two at a time to speak for a second in low tones to his next caller. Returning, he said, "I wish there had been time to talk to each of you individually. I believe the Indian yogas offer much that could help some of you in the recovery process of working through the Twelve Steps and only wish I could do more to help. If any of you will be in the City, please telephone ahead, and I will set aside some time. Meanwhile, I hope these tapes will be of help if you decide to try meditation. Incidentally, the best time is early morning after rising, before the mind has a chance to get involved with the world around it.

"Be sure to give my best to Dr. Miller," he said; "Bob telephoned earlier and asked me to tell you that your visit has been approved by the hospital as part of your recovery program so that all your expenses will be covered." With that Mr. Bharati shook hands and gave each of them a meditation tape as he said good-byes and escorted them to the door.

Outside in the sunlight, Charley stretched and said, "Man! How about that! I don't know how to take it all, but I think I feel a little bit of a lift. Elevated, if you know what I mean." They all nodded and laughed a little self-consciously as they started walking down the street toward Lexington Avenue and the 77th Street subway station trying to sort out their own thoughts and impressions. So it was that they began to retrace their steps away from a new, strange and somewhat mysterious experience and back to the more familiar, forbidding realities of the rehab center.

CHAPTER NINE
Doubleheader

It was early in the morning, 5:45 to be exact. Since returning from New York City five days ago Charley had gotten up early enough to do some push ups and play Mr. Bharati's meditation tape before joining his colleagues for breakfast.

This morning, before doing anything else, he was standing on his head, close to a wall for back-up. He had cradled the back of his head between the palms of his hands, fingers interlocked, and gently walked up on his toes to a point where he was almost balanced on his head. With a little shove, he elevated smoothly into the jack-knife position where he remained until his balance was secure. Then gently and smoothly, maintaining his center of balance, he lifted his legs into a full headstand. It was a piece of cake. Charley had mastered the technique long ago in high school where he'd been something of a gymnast and yesterday, in thumbing idly through the yellowing pages of a book on hatha yoga he'd accidentally stumbled across in the fourth floor library, he'd found himself looking at a drawing of a yogi doing the headstand. The benefits promised were too good to be missed: "Sends increased blood supply to brain, pineal body and pituitary gland—

benefits cardiac and digestive systems
tones up the nervous system
helps remove headaches, dizziness, and arterio-sclerosis
improves intelligence and memory
treats the degeneration of nerve centers
benefits liver, spleen, sexual degeneration
hernia and visceroptosis treated
relieves asthmatic discomfort."[1]

Charley had thought he wouldn't mind any or all of the above, but not hoping for miracles, mostly thought that a minute or two on his head might clear it nicely for meditation. Also, he wondered if Mr. Bharati stood on his head. He'd heard that movie stars did it to keep their good looks. That might be why Mr. Bharati always looked so young and fit.

After two or three minutes, Charley began to feel a little shaky upside down and eased himself slowly again into the jack-knife position before gently lowering himself to the floor. Not bad for a recovering alcoholic and coke addict, he thought, as he sat up and prepared for another attempt at meditation. At least he hadn't gotten into crack. That could have really loused him up for good. Something to be thankful for he thought to himself, thinking positively as the recovery experts recommended.

This morning he was going to try to meditate without the tape. He had been able, he suspected because he had long legs, to sit in the easy posture right from the beginning, although he felt restless at times and had some difficulty sitting upright as the 25-30 minute tape ran its course. Everyday the posture was becoming more comfortable and natural to him so that at times he altogether forgot that he was sitting in a strange position for a Westerner. He couldn't say with 100% certainty that he felt better, but he thought he sensed, however dimly, a realm of experience and consciousness beyond anything he had imagined. He knew he wanted to continue, to see what would happen. Also he knew he was feeling more receptive to and less critical of the NA and AA meetings and the people who attended them. Who knows, it's possible that he would be able to gain faith in a higher power, perhaps even the illusive and tantalizing one that was part of Mr. Bharati's meditation.

Cautiously easing himself into the easy posture, Charley straightened his back, closed his eyes and chanted Om, Om, Om to himself several times. He remembered the simple Sanskrit prayer that Mr. Bharati used on the tape:

> Lead us from the unreal to the real.
> Lead us from darkness to light.
> Lead us from death to Immortal Being.

O Divine One! You are the spirit of manifestation,
Manifest yourself in us,
And protect us ever by your auspicious face.

What "auspicious face" Charley wondered? But he went on chanting to himself Om, Om, Om . . .

He proceeded as best he could with the steps in Mr. Bharati's meditation. Feeling that the body was pure as a crystal; fresh soft, supple as a fresh blown flower; clean, healthy and strong in every part.

He breathed in and out imagining that a radiant stream of energy was purifying and relaxing his body. He sent thoughts of love out in all directions and prayed to all the illumined saints of the past and present and most of all to his Innermost Self for light and guidance, wisdom and strength. He tried to distance himself from his physical being, observing all his thoughts and actions as they passed by, but remaining the unattached, unaffected, unchanging witness.

Charley sat in silence watching and waiting, mentally repeating Om, Om, Om . . .

Presently he breathed in and imagined a current flowing down his spine to the base, striking at the dormant energy lying there. As he breathed out he tried to feel the current rising up his spine to the heart area along the spine and opening up the center of Truth and Understanding at the source of his being. He visualized a luminous light touching his heart, a luminous ocean of peace and bliss; he was immersed in this ocean, dissolving in it. Charley concentrated his mind on this light in the heart center and continued on the repetition of Om, Om, Om . . . Om, Om, Om . . . Om, Om, Om . . .

As Charley sat, his mind would wander and stray. Once he found himself thinking about the breakfast menu, another time about a meeting with his social worker that he shouldn't forget, and again whether Mr. Bharati would approve of what he was doing. Each time his thoughts strayed, he brought his mind back as gently as possible to the heart area to renew concentration on the luminous ocean of light and resumed again his inward chant of Om, Om, Om . . .

Some time had passed when Charley recalled the mysterious and seemingly hypnotic ending to Mr. Bharati's chanting at the deepest part of meditation and Charley intoned Om Ramakrishna, Om Ramakrishna several times and fell into a state of silence for four or five minutes, barely breathing at all.

When the moment seemed right, he began to take a few deep breaths and felt himself returning to his seat on the floor in his room feeling refreshed and restored, healthy and strong, calm and relaxed.

That's some beautiful process, Charley half-hummed to himself, as he untwined his legs and stretched them out waiting for circulation to return. It'll take a lot of practice and a lot of time, but I want to keep at it. I feel it's right, that's what really important.

All the same, as Patty asked the other day in New York, I keep wondering if there aren't easier ways to realize a higher power that I might practice as well as meditation. I know Mr. Bharati mentioned the way of love briefly. But love of any kind has never been one of my long suits, perhaps because I've never been sure exactly what it is. It's one of those words that a lot of self-righteous people fling around and don't have the slightest notion of what they're talking about. If I use the word at all, I want to be honest about it, and that's hard to do.

Also thinking of mysteries, I wonder what's happened to my old friend of these rehab days, that ancient voice that ran about in my head. More and more it seems to me that the voice said things awfully close to what Mr. Bharati quoted from the Bhagavad Gita. He's been silent for a long time, since before our trip to New York. Could be he's like the genie in Aladdin and his magic lamp and that I've used up all the visitations I'm entitled to. Should I give the lamp another rub? I'll bet he'd have something honest to say about love.

Apparently taking this for an invitation, although it wasn't all that clear that Charley meant it as such, the voice of the ancient wise one again began to speak:

> O Inquiring Charley! I shall now tell you, who is without cavil, the most secret wisdom, together with how to realize it, knowing which you will be free from evil.
> This is the king of knowledge, king of secrets, pure and best, and directly perceptible. It is easy to practice and imperishable.

He's back! Here we go again thought Charley, rather pleased and still sitting on the floor. This time he's off in a different direction. Could it be the Greek mysteries? They were secret but I doubt that they were easy to practice. Anyway, I was wondering about easier ways to practice. The old voice may be answering my thoughts. So let's hear about it, O Wise and Potent Oracle! thought Charley in fond and familiar jest. I won't tell a soul that I shouldn't.

The ancient voice was undisturbed by Charley's familiarity:

> The whole universe is pervaded by my unmanifested form; all beings abide in me, I do not abide in them. As the air which moves everywhere is in the sky, so know that all beings are in me.

Sometimes he phrases words beautifully, approved Charley. Air is in space, but you can't say it is touching space. He said before that all beings are in him but he is not in the beings. Paradox after paradox, puzzle after puzzle.

The always mysterious words continued:

> O Charley! At the end of a cycle all beings dissolve into my Nature; I project them again at the beginning of another.

> But these actions do not bind me because I stay
> detached and indifferent.

Charley was pleased to find that the old voice was practicing what it preached. Pretty neat. He's describing karma yoga where actions do not bind if you stay unattached to results. He seems to say the same thing over and over, but in different ways. I guess he hopes it'll sink in sooner or later.

The voice continued its revelations:

> Under my supervision Nature produces the living and
> the non-living. The world goes in cycles of creation and
> destruction by reason of this.
> The dull-witted, without knowledge of my supreme
> status as the Great Lord of beings, disregard me
> incarnated in human form.

Charley couldn't help thinking about Divine Incarnations. The voice is saying again that he becomes incarnations such as Jesus, Krishna in the Gita, Buddha, he thought. And Dr. Miller said many considered Ramakrishna to be one. I doubt that I'd be able to recognize one if I saw one. But if Mr. Bharati was taught by one of Ramakrishna's disciples, that's like being sort of close to a higher power I'd guess.

Ignoring these speculations, the voice resumed:

> These people are of vain hopes, of vain deeds, of vain
> knowledge and without sense. They are possessed of
> ghoulish and demoniac natures.
> But, O My Inquiring Charley! the great-souled ones
> who have the divine nature, knowing me, the
> Imperishable Source of beings, worship me with single-
> minded devotion.

He could be talking about unwavering concentration thought Charley such as you need for meditation. Or more likely he's referring to the persistent effort and stick-to-itiveness you seem to need to develop faith in a higher power. "Single-minded" love and devotion don't seem to come easy, especially when your mind is cluttered by TV and newspapers and held in sway by the distractions of the world of today. I'm still waiting for that fair wind of grace that Ramakrishna talked about. Without that, it's an almost impossible trip. At least that's what my poor, eroded intuition tells me.

The voice had more to say about love and devotion:

> Singing my name always, striving with firm vows and bowing down to me with devotion, the great-souled ones worship me constantly.

When he says "singing my name" it could be like the young Hare Krishnas singing and dancing on the streets of New York City. Or could he mean Om, Om, Om . . . wondered Charley? Bet it could be either, or both, he thought, remembering the young Hare Krishna's advice to take his choice, anyway he'd like.

But the inscrutable voice went on:

> And others worship me, the All-facing, with the sacrifice of knowledge. Some worship me as the One, some as the Distinct, and some as the Manifold.

There he goes again, thought Charley. He says he can be anything and everything in the world, that the world is God alone. God covers whatever exists. That's hardly an easy concept to grasp; I'm not at all sure I have it straight.

The voice continued to describe itself in new ways:

> I am the father of this world, its mother, protector and grandfather. I am also all that is to be known, all that is pure, the Om and all the scriptures.
> I am the way, the sustainer, the Lord, the witness, the abode, the refuge, the friend, the origin, the dissolution, the ground, the death and the Eternal Seed.

> Those who worship me think of me as their own. For them who are thus always united with me, I bring what they need and secure what they have.

He never seems far from the Twelve Steps, thought Charley. He says he takes care of those who rely on him completely, which is what you'd have to hope for in turning your will and your life over to the care of God in Step Two. One minute I seem to grasp these things, the next minute they elude me, but then, I don't think I'm the only one with this problem. I think almost everyone has some doubts about turning everything over to God unless they have complete faith and devotion.

The voice continued to explain:

> O Charley! Even those devotees who worship other gods with faith worship me alone, though without knowledge.

Well it seems the "as I understand Him" clause of Step Two is OK and that the many different divinities are powers of One God. That kind of makes sense to me, Charley concurred thoughtfully, as the image of Mickey Mouse or even the Easter Bunny as a kind of divinity flickered through his head with gentle humor.

The omnipotent voice went on:

> The worshippers of gods go to gods, the worshippers of the ancestors go to the ancestors, the worshippers of spirits go to spirits, while my worshippers come to me. O Charley! Whatever you do, whatever you eat, whatever you sacrifice, whatever you donate and whatever austerity you practice, offer it to me. You will thus be free from the bondage of action, its good and bad results, and being free because of renunciation of the results of action, you will come to me.

As more and more Charley felt he had some understanding and comprehension, however uncertain, of what the ancient old voice was saying, he became aware that the voice was fading and becoming more distant in his head. He strained to hear as the voice continued:

> I am the same to all beings, none is hateful or dear to me. But those who worship me with love are in me and I am also in them.
> Even if a person of the most outrageous conduct worships me with single-minded devotion, he is to be regarded as holy, for he is rightly resolved.
> He quickly becomes a righteous soul and attains eternal peace. O Charley! Know for certain a devotee of mine never perishes.[2]

With these words of promise and hope for everyone, the ancient old voice faded completely away into the inner-most recesses of Charley's head. Oh, Oh! thought Charley, I've lost contact just when the voice said that even if a person like me, "of the most outrageous conduct," worships the Supreme Spirit with devotion he is rightly resolved and quickly attains eternal peace. What a great, wonderful wide-open promise. That must be the mysterious secret: love and devotion. Easy to practice if you keep at it, and anyone can do it, even totally messed-up addicts like me and the rest of us here at the rehab center.

Charley strained again to see if he could hear the ancient one, and for a moment thought he heard it say in a faint, faint whisper:

> Dwell on me, be my devotee, worship me and bow down to me. Having thus taken refuge in me and uniting your heart with me, you will come to me alone.[3]

I wonder if the voice is gone for good thought Charley as he got up from his seat on the floor and started to dress for the day. It said some wonderful things, even if for a while I was really worried about hearing it. Now I'll miss it, but I think I know where it might have been coming from, and I'm really feeling so much better and hopeful that I feel thankful to have heard it. It was faint praise, but coming from the depths of the recovery that was slowly taking form for Charley, it meant a lot.

CHAPTER TEN

The Package

The four of them, Patty, Mary, Samson and Charley, had eaten lunch together and were now relaxing in the lounge area, talking and laughing with easy familiarity. Their visit to Mr. Bharati's studio in New York seemed to bind them together, and they often went to substance abuse meetings together as well as socializing at meals and once even getting a pass for an excursion to the movies.

Of the four, there most obviously had been a change in Mary. She no longer seemed gray and lackluster. She stood straighter, her face had lost much of its pallor, and her eyes and face were alert and interested in their surroundings. Samson and Patty were much the same, one strong and shining, the other unsteady but vibrant and often very entertaining. Outwardly less noticeable, there also had been a change in Charley. He was less angry, more self-assured and calm and somehow had an aura of strength and even power about himself that the others had begun to sense when they were with him. Once when they were off by themselves for a moment, Mary told Charley that she had played Mr. Bharati's tape several times. She didn't know how long she would keep using it and had no plans really about it. She simply knew it was giving her support that she needed desperately. The others, Charley was almost certain, had put their tapes aside for another day. They were far from negative about their visit to Mr. Bharati, but meditation really, darling, wasn't their cup of tea, as Patty no doubt would have phrased it.

Without giving it much thought, Charley said, "You know, the other night coming home from the movies I noticed several posters put up around town showing an Indian yogi, Sri Agananda, playing a cello and inviting one and all to a big Peace Festival next week at the Civic Center. Maybe we should go if we're all still here. I can guarantee you it would be a different kind of experience than our visit to Mr. Bharati." The others looked interested, and Charley continued, "I'm not good at telling stories, but let me try to tell you about my strange, literally illuminating experience with Sri Agananda a couple of years ago."

Patty, Mary and Samson grinned in agreement and sat back comfortably in their chairs to listen as Charley began:

"I have, or probably should say had, an artist friend, Sam Jewel, who used to do mechanicals and finished art for some of the accounts I handled. Sam used to do drugs and drink like the rest of the gang and was about to go off the deep end when he somehow or other stumbled upon a swami, Sri Agananda, who turned his life from a shambles into peace and order. Sam became a different person, secure, serene, very reliable and tremendously creative. Sri, as I came to call him, gave Sam a new name, Balaram, and picked out a wife for Sam from among his female disciples. I think Sam gave him every cent he made. The followers lived in a spotless tenement off Second Avenue down toward the Village, and Sam would talk and talk about how great and talented the swami, Guru he called him, was and how he wanted to take me to one of Sri's appearances which were usually advertised with posters plastered all over the city wherever there was an empty space. He said Guru had taken up painting and had painted heavenly splashes for twenty-four hours non-stop. He also said Guru was a superb, unrecognized musician playing Eastern and Western instruments. Guru was also a poet, and he gave me some amateurish samples printed on a home press. At one point the disciples were hell-bent on nominating Sri for a Nobel Prize and were certain he'd get it. Much to his credit, I must add that he held weekly meditations in the small chapel at the United Nations that were attended by some of the delegates and were open to the general public as well.

"You can see the kind of enthusiasm I had to listen to. It was soft, but persistent and full of worship. As gently as I could, I kept putting Sam off for months, but finally I gave in and agreed to go with him to one of Sri's appearances scheduled on a Sunday afternoon, when I was likely to have a fairly clear head, at Hunter College auditorium.

"I was to meet Sam, or Balaram as he now preferred to be called, in the lobby of the auditorium. When I arrived the place was filled with some civilians like myself and what must of been a couple of hundred disciples, all dressed in white shirts and pants or white dresses and each wearing a single red rose. I asked a beatific usher if he knew where Balaram might be and was told he was back stage for a moment and that I should take a seat in the auditorium and wait for him. This I did, and in a few minutes Balaram showed up rose-adorned and neatly dressed in white. He smiled happily and sat down next to me to wait for the proceedings to begin. He said he'd been backstage helping Guru get dressed which I gathered was a big honor or privilege.

"After a bit the curtain went up, revealing a huge, high-backed golden throne at the center of the stage. It was softly lit in gently changing colors. When the audience was settled and quiet Sri Agananda appeared dressed in a floor length, flowing, translucent orange gown. He was six feet or so tall, had a sharp nose, shaved head and light brown skin. From time to time, the pupils of his eyes tended to disappear upwards under his eyelids, which was a little disconcerting. He walked over to the throne, turned and faced the audience and with the palms of his hands pressed together saluted them in all directions, left, right, center and above in the balcony. Sri said a few very slowly spaced words of welcome in what turned out to be an unexpectedly thin, scratchy voice, then turned and sat on the heavily cushioned throne. He repeated 'Om' three times, let the pupils of his eyes disappear and sat motionless before the audience with the lights changing colors slowly on his presence.

"Soon began more than an hour-long procession of musicians playing sitars, violin, cello, piano, jazz guitar, synthesizer, you name it. One or two were well-known professionals who were disciples of Sri Agananda. They were all first-rate.

The Package

Meanwhile, most of the audience kept their eyes expectantly transfixed on Sri who never seemed to move an inch. I followed suit, although I managed to keep track of the musicians and what they were playing. With those lights playing on Sri, it was hard to say what was happening, but he seemed to change faces in it, going from an old man to a young man, from light to dark, once even I could have sworn he assumed a monkey's face. Sam, or rather Balaram, was sitting there with his eyes glued on Sri and beaming. I wasn't sure what he was seeing.

"Then what I gather was the grand finale occurred. A pristine looking women's chorus of disciples was on stage surrounding Sri Agananda and singing a simplistic devotional song about Love and the Supreme, whatever that was supposed to mean. It was really irritating and boring, although the choir's vocal work was OK. I was looking at Sri, when all at once the stage, chorus and Sri disappeared in a blaze of white light. I heard Sam mutter, 'Wow!' and assumed I wasn't alone in this mirage, if that's what it was. It was really astonishing. In a moment, things returned to normal with all present and accounted for. I wondered at what I'd seen, but I didn't feel any better or worse for the experience. If I'd seen a miraculous demonstration of spiritual power, it held no meaning for me. My reaction was pretty much, 'How about that? So what?' To my unenlightened eye, it was sort of like having seen a magician perform a grand illusion. Sam, on the other hand, was obviously in another world and joyous at this fantastic performance.

"As a wind-up everyone in the audience was invited to come on stage and receive spiritual food in the form of an orange from the hands of Sri Agananda. I went up with Sam and imitated his salute to Sri with hands pressed, palms together, and took my orange feeling more than a little embarrassed, but not wanting to upset Sam.

"Afterwards, I said thanks and good-bye and Sam went off to more backstage duties. I ate the orange as I walked back to my mid-town apartment. It was good, but nothing supernatural occurred as it passed through my system that I could notice, no cleansing diarrhea or anything like that.

"While I remained curious about Sri Agananda and felt an almost superstitious respect for him, I wasn't drawn to him as a teacher or guide, especially one who would choose a wife for me, tell me when I could have sex and strictly rule my life the way Sam's life was ruled. As I said, it was an interesting experience and to this day, I don't know whether what I saw was the result of spiritual power, hallucination on my part or very clever stage lighting."

Charley looked a little shy as he said, "That's my recitation for today, folks. It's more words than I've put together in a long time, and about things I haven't thought about for a long time that actually might relate somehow to the problems I'm having with AA and NA in accepting a higher power. Anyway, if we can make it, it might be fun to go and see what Sri Agananda is up to these days at the Peace Festival."

Patty, who had been listening carefully, leaned forward and said, "I don't personally know anything about such things, Charley, but I do know from some writing research I did a while back that occult powers such as you might have been describing are not always considered to be proof of spiritual advancement and are considered by many to be potential roadblocks to spiritual progress. There was a famous renegade monk by the name of Rasputin in Russia not too long ago who almost ruled the royal family and still has people talking about the evil he caused and how he survived poisoning and drowning with his mysterious powers. That isn't to say that Sri Agananda isn't a wonderful influence on his disciples, but the subject is a really fascinating one, don't you think?"

Samson, who had never heard of Rasputin and liked the name, was just starting to ask Patty more about him when one of the ever-present attendants came up to them with a thick extra-large manila envelope addressed to Charley. Charley was surprised. He was expecting no package from anyone. It was addressed in an unfamiliar hand and Charley spotted a New

The Package

York City postmark. A little embarrassed at having become the center of attention and curiosity, Charley took the package and hastily excused himself, saying that he'd be back in a few minutes and started off in the direction of his room.

In the privacy of his room, Charley looked more closely at the package and saw that it came from Mr. Bharati's address. He was filled with anticipation and a feeling of excitement. Shortly after returning from New York City, Charley had found a time when he felt pretty much together and had read through the print-out of Mr. Bharati's translation and commentary on Karma Yoga, or the Yoga of Action, of the Bhagavad Gita. He was impressed with it and thought it might well help him in his work on the Twelve Steps. Again, he also was almost certain that the voice in his head had said very similar words to him, and he wanted a copy of the Gita on hand to read and study when he had the time, strength and attention span for it. So Charley had taken the pad of yellow-lined legal paper he had left over from his days in the advertising business, and penned a short double-spaced note to Mr. Bharati:

> Dear Mr. Bharati,
> Thank you for seeing Patty, Mary, Samson and myself last Saturday afternoon. We all felt our visit was rewarding.
> I have played your meditation tape several times and hope to continue practicing meditation. After I leave this place and get settled, I hope to telephone you to arrange for a time to see you again for more instruction and discussion.
> Since returning, I have read your Chapter on Karma Yoga from the Gita that you left after your lecture here and would very much like to obtain a copy of the complete work. Could you tell me where the book is available? I hate to bother you, but no information is given on the print-out.
> Sincerely,
> Charley, the recovering addict

Charley tore the thick padded envelope open like a five year old kid opening a Christmas present. Inside was a spiral bound volume of more than two hundred typewritten pages with a blue cardboard cover on which was printed:

> THE BHAGAVAD GITA
> (THE DIVINE SONG)
> Translated from Sanskrit
> with Introduction and Comments by
> Keshab Bharati

Clipped to the cover was a handwritten letter from Mr. Bharati. Concentrating on Mr. Bharati's smooth flowing but unfamiliar script, Charley slowly began to decipher the letter. It read:

Dear Charley,

I was honored to have you and your friends visit my studio. I hope your journey home was safe and that your visit helped you all in one way or another toward recovery.

When you are ready, I will be glad to have you visit. I hope that arrangements will go smoothly for you when you leave the hospital.

I'm glad that you found time and strength to read the chapter on karma yoga. The book is not yet available, as several publishers are now considering it. However, I do have an extra copy of the manuscript and want you to have it. I hope it will be useful to you. It would be good if you could read a few verses of it early every morning before you meditate.

Please give my regards to Patty, Mary, Samson and Dr. Miller should you see them.

Sincerely,
Keshab Bharati

Charley was tremendously pleased and flattered that Mr. Bharati should send a manuscript copy for him to read. No grass grows under his feet, Charley thought, reverting back to the cliches of his boyhood in Ohio. Charley picked up the book and let it fall open at random. I'll see what the message is for today he thought as he unconsciously started a game he'd often played using Gideon Bibles in hotel rooms.

The Gita had fallen open to the beginning of chapter 18 entitled, "The Yoga Of Liberation." It was the last chapter of the book. Charley began to read Mr. Bharati's opening remarks:

> This last chapter of the Gita summarizes its teachings. The Gita is a book of conduct. Life is a matter of conduct in all the various branches of its expression as well as in the orientation to its ultimate goal. Ethics and religion are not separate as it has been thought by many thinkers in the West including theologians. God is Good. The ideal of morality is never realized fully in action in the relative world. It is however realized within, in feeling as the height of spiritual experience. Ethics points to this goal.
> A civilized society with its various functions and relationships has the ideal of duty. However its correct performance is not easy unless duty is greased with love and becomes true obligation to Truth. This duty does not cancel other duties; it includes them but excludes pursuits which hurt integrity. When all activities are performed with dedication to Truth, life becomes religious. When it is realized that Truth is the essence of our personality which is also love, freedom and bliss, the concept of duty melts into the spirit of worship. It is through erosion of the shadow-self that we advance toward our true Self which is eternal life.
> Such a transformation of life happens through faith and worship. The Gita delivers this perennial message in an unparalleled manner.

He really writes well, thought Charley, and I think I follow most of it. If only I can put some of it into practice, I think I might be able to work my way out of the mess I've gotten myself into. Let's see what Arjuna and Lord Krishna are talking about for eleven lucky verses:

Arjuna said:
O Mighty-Armed One! O Lord of the Senses and O Destroyer of Keshi (a demon)! I want to know respectively the truth about abandonment of works and also of renunciation.
The Blessed Lord said:
The learned declare the renunciation of actions with desire to be abandonment (*sannyasa*); the sagacious say that renunciation of results of works is relinquishment.

Action should be given up as an evil say some philosophers; while others say acts of sacrifice, gift and austerity should never be given up.

O Best among the Descendants of Bharata (Arjuna) and Tiger among Men! Hear from me the final truth about renunciation, for renunciation has been declared to be threefold.

Acts of sacrifice, charity and austerity should not be given up but ought to be performed, for sacrifice, gift and austerity are purifying for the discerning.

Even these acts are to be performed giving up attachment and the desire for results—this is my certain and mature conviction.

Renunciation of duty that has been enjoined is not proper; its relinquishment through delusion is declared to be stupid (*tamasic*).

He who gives up work out of fear of physical hardship, thus performing tainted (*rajasic*) renunciation only, will not reap the fruit of renunciation.

> O Arjuna! When a prescribed action is performed without attachment and the desire for results, that renunciation is called pure (*sattvic*).
>
> The man of renunciation endowed with serenity of mind (*sattva*), wise and with his doubts dispelled does not hate a disagreeable action nor is he attached to an agreeable one.
>
> Because it is not possible for an embodied being to give up action altogether, he who gives up the results of action is called a man of renunciation.[1]

So be it! thought Charley. As the Gita says, a man of renunciation must I try to be, giving up attachment and the desire for results, turning all that over to the care of God as Step Two tells me to do. And it also says that "the man of renunciation" is endowed with serenity which reminds me of the Serenity Prayer they repeat at the meetings:

> God grant me the serenity
> To accept the things I cannot change,
> Courage to change the things I can.
> And wisdom to know the difference.

That's the message for today, folks! All brought to you by the Grand Casino of Chance located on the boardwalk of life not far from your hometown.

Seriously though, thought Charley, if I could ever get past Step Two, the Twelve Steps would be a lot easier. Some of them involve list making, taking inventory. That'd be interesting if the things I'd have to list weren't so devastating. Hurting people, probably killing some. Try as I might, most of the wrongs I've committed can never be righted; but I think they could be left behind if I can manage to go ahead with the right attitude toward what's left of my life. What's the slogan? "Today is the first day of the rest of my life."

Well the past is all water over the dam, or under the

bridge as Mother used to say, and I'm going to have to start life all over again when I get out of here; however, for the time-being I'm here and I'll have to make the best of it. Looking at his watch Charley realized that time had flown by and he was late for an appointment with his psychiatrist Dr. Shaw. Fifteen minutes late, that's $25 worth gone forever thought Charley as he started out the door.

CHAPTER ELEVEN

Talk About Coincidence

Charley was sitting on a comfortable sofa in an alcove facing one of the main marble corridors of the hospital. He was a few minutes early for an appointment he'd made with Dr. Miller and was more than a little anxious because he'd decided to ask Dr. Miller to be his psychiatrist. He also felt on pins and needles because he'd decided to tell Dr. Miller about the voice he'd heard in his head, even though he was pretty sure it had left him when it had faded away the other day. Then he smiled faintly as he remembered the famous line about General MacArthur, "Old soldiers never die, they just fade away," and some of his lingering impressions of the ancient voice wandered through his mind.

A group of about twelve teenagers passed noisily by on their way to their day work program in another part of the hospital. They were shepherded by two sharp-eyed, intelligent-looking attendants who were only a few years older than their charges. Some of the teenage group looked bright, almost too bright; some of them seemed erratic in their walk and mannerisms. A few moved along wearily and looked dejected. How many of them are in for doing drugs, wondered Charley? Quite a few, I'll bet, but there must be other problems underlying the drugs. Hope they can get out clean and get a fresh start. It's a tough world, and you really get a heart-wrenching glimpse of it here. Teenagers, young adults, middle-aged adults, old folks, you see them all here, but it hurts most to see the young kids beaten before they can get started. I wonder if they have a Twelve Step Program for kids. Probably do. I think they have them nowadays for gamblers, over-eaters, under-eaters and you name it! Even for suffering parents and friends of the afflicted, or the diseased as you could call us. It's almost become a fad kind of thing. I hope it doesn't become too much of a good thing and run out of gas. Not likely though, people never stop wanting to tell others about their troubles. Could be that's what keeps the meetings going on and on, sometimes to the point of excruciating boredom. That must be one of the reasons they always say, "Keep coming back, keep coming back." I think they really must mean, "Don't give up the ship, don't give up the ship."

Charley's nervous musings were interrupted when a door of one of the nearby offices opened. Dr. Miller appeared, and with a welcoming hand and smile said, "Come in, Charley, it's good to see you. You're looking great, much better than a couple of weeks ago. Please have a seat."

Dr. Miller ushered Charley into his office and gestured toward a comfortable black-leather chair. The room seemed quiet and relaxing with photographs of serene Western desert scenes on the walls, soft light and a beautiful Oriental rug on the floor. Charley sat down, crossed his legs, leaned back, took a deep breath and felt pretty much at ease.

"What can I do for you Charley?" asked Dr. Miller from his desk chair several feet away. He folded his hands together and leaned slightly forward as he threw the ball into Charley's court. Charley cleared his throat and began, with some obvious uncertainty, to talk.

"I wanted to see you for several reasons," he said. "I'm not sure all this will come out the way I'd like it to," he continued, "but I'll be leaving here in a week or so, and I'm going to need some help for a few weeks or months to keep straight. I don't think I'll make it strictly on my own. Also, as you may have guessed, after hearing and visiting Mr. Bharati, I've gotten interested in some of the yogas and meditation and I want to learn more about these things. Well," Charley cleared his throat again and hesitated for a second, "I've been seeing Dr. Shaw who was assigned to me when I was admitted to the rehab unit, and he's honestly tried to be helpful. But he's so straight it hurts, and he's a total blank when it comes to Indian philosophy, knows nothing about it and admits it. I think he's a good old-fashioned High-Church Episcopalian. Nothing wrong with that except it sort of blocks our line of communications. Sometimes our points of view are miles, or maybe I should say continents, apart." Charley paused again, and getting no response other than an encouraging look from Dr. Miller, went haltingly on, "To make a long story short, I'd like to ask you to see me once or even twice a week from now on until I can get to feel more sure of myself."

Dr. Miller said, "I see no problem with that, Charley. I'd like very much to work with you, and Dr. Shaw is a very capable professional man whom I'm sure will be disappointed, but will also understand."

"I should tell you," Dr. Miller resumed, "that my approach is different from most of my colleagues in that it's based on Jungian principles. Without going into much detail this means that my thinking is influenced by Jung's concept of a collective or racial unconscious operating in each of us. This comes into play in the Jungian interpretation of dreams and fantasies in which the symbols which occur suggest that at the very deepest level we share an unconscious common to all of us or, as Jung called it, a collective unconscious. In his autobiography Jung describes a fantasy figure whom he called Philemon with whom he held mental conversations in which Philemon said things which had never passed through Jung's conscious mind, leading him to the conclusion that there are things in the psyche which have their own life and exist as images from our common racial unconscious.[1]

Charley's eyes were about to pop out of his head, but before he could interrupt, Dr. Miller continued on, "Jung was interested in Eastern philosophy. You'll be surprised to know that Mr. Bharati met him many years ago when Jung visited the monastery of the Ramakrishna Mission in India around the time when a big temple of Ramakrishna was being dedicated. He felt the truth of religious need deeply and honestly.

"Now," Dr. Miller concluded, "you'll come to know more of Jung's theories as we go along, and we'll have time to talk about many things from time to time; however, you may have some matters you'd like to bring up today. If you do, fire away."

Charley tried to collect himself as he said, "Some of what you've already said is almost too much of a coincidence. The main reason I wanted to see you was to tell you about a voice I've had floating around in my head that may not be too far afield from the one Jung talked to. I think it's gone now, but I can't be sure. It first came on loud and clear a day or so after I checked in here. I was feeling desperate and about ready to slit my throat when this strange, ancient-sounding voice began to speak in the back of my head. It said things such as, 'I am the light in the sun and the moon, I am the origin and source of all beings, the intelligence of the intelligent,' and so on. It sounded like God speaking, and I was very much in need of a God. I didn't know what to think, and I didn't want to tell anyone around here about it, that's for sure.

"The voice came back several times, telling me how to act without desire for results and how to turn my life over into the hands of a higher power, even saying I could choose any power I wanted, although it seemed to suggest that the voice itself would be the best choice. Much of what the voice said fit into the Twelve Step program like pieces in a jigsaw puzzle and helped me find meetings more acceptable and useful. Once it came to me in a dream, and I found myself in an almost identical situation to that which I heard Mr. Bharati describe a few days later when he told about Krishna talking to Arjuna on the battlefield between two opposing armies of relatives and friends. About the only difference was that my battlefield was in Vietnam not long ago and Arjuna's was in India several thousand years ago.

"After hearing Mr. Bharati talk, I was pretty sure that what the voice was saying to me was extremely close to what Krishna said to Arjuna in the Gita. Futhermore, it seemed to be helping me. I was feeling better about myself and more able to tolerate and attempt to understand the others. The voice talked to me about meditation, and at my request, you arranged for the four of us to see Mr. Bharati in New York City. I wanted to know about faith and devotion, which I lack sure as hell, and like the genie from Aladdin and his lamp, the voice came through again, but this time, it started fading in and out and finally disappeared into the void, saying something like:

> Dwell on me, be my devotee, worship me, take refuge in me, unite your heart in me and you will come to me alone.

"I haven't heard from it in more than a week. I think it's gone. In the meantime, Mr. Bharati sent me a manuscript copy of his new translation and commentary on the Gita, and from what I've read, I'm certain, although I'll never be able to prove it, that the voice in my head was reciting verses from the Gita, or a reasonable facsimile of it. I'm very grateful to that old voice, but I know that what's been going through my head as though on a tape recording is hardly normal, and I wanted to tell you about it because I thought if anyone around here could understand, it would be you."

Dr. Miller had been silent and very intent on what Charley had been saying. He said, "Well, as you heard me say a minute ago, even Jung had mental conversations with a voice. His Philemon, as he called his voice, was a mysterious figure with superior insight who at times seemed quite real, like a living personality. He even used to walk up and down in the garden with him. Philemon seemed so real to Jung that he considered him to be what the Indians call a guru.[2]

"Someday, Charley, you may come to think of your ancient voice in the same light. Time will tell. One thing is pretty certain, your voice sounds like a beneficient one coming from deep inside yourself at a time of great personal need. These are things that happen that we can't explain with any certainty, but it helps a little to know that someone as great as Jung valued them and took them seriously.

"While you've probably had a fortunate, if inexplicable experience, I want to add a word of caution: voices, as you probably know, have been known to tell people to take some very dangerous actions. If your voice comes back, please get in touch with me immediately, and we'll talk it over right away while the words are fresh in your mind. I wouldn't fret over it, and I wouldn't discuss it with anyone, as there's really nothing to be gained by spreading it around. Most people would not understand, or I should say could even be expected to misunderstand; they quickly distance themselves from anything unfamiliar to their everyday world.

"Thank you, Charley, for telling me about your voice. It was a most unusual experience that perhaps you'll treasure as the years go by.

"Come to think of it," said Dr. Miller, pausing as though he'd thought of something important, "there's an exception to what I just said about not discussing your voice in the head with anyone. If you feel up to it, I would suggest that you write Mr. Bharati about it. You might be surprised and helped by what he might have to say. His approach is beyond medicine and science, superscience he sometimes calls it, and I must admit that I often feel there is much to be said for it, although as a practitioner of psychiatry and medicine I necessarily stay pretty much within the bounds of what the profession accepts.

"Is there anything else you'd like to bring up today? We still have a few minutes before my next appointment."

Charley felt rather cleansed by his confession, if that's what it had been. He said, "Thank you for suggesting that I contact Mr. Bharati. I really would like to hear what he has to say about my ancient voice, and I do have at least one more question that I want to ask that's kind of related."

After pausing for a second, Charley impulsively blurted out, "Actually, make that two questions, Dr. Miller! I hadn't intended to bring this up, but I told Samson, Patty and Mary about this strange episode I had with Sri Agananda, who is sort of an Indian yogi cult figure in New York City, and it's been on my mind ever since. To make a long story short, an artist friend of mine talked me into going to one of Sri's public appearances at Hunter College. Well, I sat through the thing, which consisted mostly of Sri sitting motionless on a throne in the center of the stage with soft colored lights playing over him and some really good musical performances by his disciples. Then at the end, something very weird happened. Sri was sitting there, surrounded by a bland singing chorus of twenty or so girls in white, when suddenly, right before my eyes, the whole stage disappeared or dissolved into a brilliant white light. A few seconds later, the light disappeared and Sri and his entourage emerged unharmed. It might have been a lighting trick, but I don't really think it was. I didn't feel any after-effects, good or bad, but I've had a lasting curiosity about what happened that afternoon. Do you think I might have seen a demonstration of occult power, or something like that?"

Dr. Miller looked a little amused. "Charley," he said, "I have no idea what it was you saw. There's good reason to believe that occult powers exist, but they're not in my bag of tricks. If I were you, I wouldn't overly concern myself about the incident. While something like this is intriguing, it can also be distracting; I certainly wouldn't worry about it. Goodness knows, right now you have more important things to tackle."

Charley smiled sheepishly and said, "Guess you're right on there, Dr. Miller." Charley rubbed the side of his nose with his forefinger and with some hesitation went on with his second question, "When you introduced Mr. Bharati at the lecture, you said that he had studied under disciples of Ramakrishna, and then Mr. Bharati began his lecture with a quotation from a book about Ramakrishna that talked about all doubts disappearing when a seeker meets a favorable wind, meaning the grace of God. Can you recall the name of the book and tell me where I might find a copy?"

Dr. Miller looked pleased as he reached to a bookshelf behind his desk and extracted a big volume. He said, "The book is *The Gospel of Sri Ramakrishna* and you can arrange to have a copy sent to you by calling the Ramakrishna-Vivekananda Center in New York City. You can get the number from information, the Center is located in the East 90s. For the time being, I'll gladly loan you my copy. Let me read a little of the foreword to you so that you won't be unduly surprised when you look into it. The foreword is by Aldous Huxley:[3]

"M", as the author modestly styles himself . . . produced a book unique, so far as my knowledge goes, in the literature of hagiography. No other saint has had so able and indefatigable a Boswell. Never have the small events of a contemplative's daily life been described with such a wealth of intimate detail. Never have the casual and unstudied utterances of a great religious teacher been set down with so minute a fidelity. To Western readers, it is true, this fidelity and this wealth of detail are sometimes a trifle disconcerting; for the social, religious and intellectual frames of reference within which Sri Ramakrishna did his thinking and expressed his feelings were entirely Indian. But after the first few surprises and bewilderments, we begin to find something peculiarly stimulating and instructive about the very strangeness and, to our eyes, the eccentricity of the man revealed to us in "M's" narrative. What a scholastic philosopher would call the "accidents" of Ramakrishna's life were intensely Hindu and therefore, so far as we in the West are concerned, unfamiliar and hard to understand; its "essence", however, was intensely mystical and therefore universal. To read through these conversations in which mystical doctrine alternates with an unfamiliar kind of humor, and where discussions of the oddest aspects of Hindu mythology give place to the most profound and subtle utterances about the nature of Ultimate Reality, is in itself a liberal education in humility, tolerance and suspense of judgment. We must be grateful to the translator for his excellent version of a book so curious and delightful as a biographical document, so precious, at the same time, for what it teaches us of the life of the spirit.

"Have fun!" said Dr. Miller as he closed the book and rose signifying the end of the session, "It's a most remarkable, strange, yet illuminating book as you'll see for yourself when you get into it."

Dr. Miller handed the book to Charley. The two of them conferred for a moment to arrange a further appointment, then Charley shook Dr. Miller's hand and was about to turn and leave when his curiosity suddenly got the better of him, and he found himself pointing to an arresting, photograph framed in gilted bamboo on the bookshelf behind Dr. Miller. "Pardon me for asking, Dr. Miller," he said, "but who in hell is that beautiful old man with the long white beard who has been staring at me all the time we've been talking?"

Dr. Miller chuckled and seemed pleased. "Charley," he said, "you're observant today, and that's a sign that you're really beginning to feel better. That beautiful old man is the poet Rabindranath Tagore who won the Nobel Prize for Literature in 1914 and who, along with Gandhi, was one of India's best known sons. It's a Kodak "Brownie" picture that was taken in India by my wife's Uncle Julian in the 1930s. Family legend has it that Julian made several requests to see the poet and each time was refused. He persisted and finally said that he'd promise to give up drinking and smoking if the poet would see him. The poet could hardly refuse the promise and agreed to see Julian. The photograph was taken during this interview, but like many of your peers in the Strecker Unit here at the hospital, if Julian kept his promise, it wasn't for long, because he was smoking Pall Malls and drinking Imperial whiskey until the day he died at the age of eighty-two. Interestingly enough, it was only after Keshab Bharati had introduced me to Tagore's poetry that I discovered to my surprise that I had been looking at Tagore's picture for many years in a gallery of photos that hung on Julian's wall.

"Tagore was a living embodiment of Indian culture, and his poems often talk with lovely simplicity of his higher power. Let me see, I think I remember one that goes like this:

> You are the Infinite playing your tune in the finite.
> That is why your revelation in me is so sweet.
> In so many colors and scents, in so many songs and rhythms,
> O the Formless One! My heart is alive with the play of your forms.

JULIAN PAPIN SCOTT

Rabindranath Tagore

"Well, I certainly hadn't intended to recite poetry today," said Dr. Miller with a slight flush of embarrassment, "but Tagore was simply incomparable. I can't resist quoting two more lines from another poem. You'll know why I remember them when I tell you that years ago, during my student days, Keshab Bharati telephoned me about them early one morning when I was barely awake. He was very excited, the way he gets sometimes, and made me listen right then and there to an old 78 rpm record from Bengal that he'd unearthed somewhere or other. It was a Tagore poem set to music and sung over an exotic rhythm background of Indian instruments. When it finished playing, before I could get a word in edgewise, he said, 'Isn't it beautiful! Listen to the words. I have translated them for you:[4]

None knows along what road you take,
    Whom, where,
But opening my eyes I suddenly discover
    That you have brought me to your door.'"

Unexpectedly, Charley thought he could see slight signs of moisture and warm, nostalgic emotion in Dr. Miller's eyes, as his new psychiatrist continued, "Mr. Bharati translates poetry into poetry wonderfully well, doesn't he, Charley? Someday, if you're interested, we'll talk more about Tagore. In the meantime, we'll just take things as they come." So saying, Dr. Miller gave Charley a friendly, departing pat on the shoulder.

Charley was pleased with Dr. Miller's willingness to drop his professional cloak to talk about Tagore in such a personal manner. He thanked him for the unexpected loan of the book on Ramakrishna and left feeling that he was carrying a wealth of riches under his arm.

As he walked down the hall toward the elevator that would take him up to the rehab quarters, Charley stopped and leaned against the wall for a moment to examine the book. It was old, but sturdy. The covers were grey cloth and all four corners, front and back, had bright yellow leather triangles for protection. He opened the front cover and found the inside lining to be a maze of white polka-dots on a faded, purplish blue background. He turned to the title page which was of paper of foreign quality that had started to turn slightly brownish and read:

THE GOSPEL OF
SRI RAMAKRISHNA
Translated by
SWAMI NIKHILANANDA
Sri Ramakrishna Math
Mylapore, Madras
India
1947

Charley turned to the illustration facing the first page. Looking out at him from the page was one of the few photographs taken of Ramakrishna. He was seated cross-legged on a cloth or towel. His face was lightly bearded, features pleasant, not handsome. His expression was serene, with a half-smile. His gaze seemed off into the distance. The upper-left edge of the page was brown from many thumb prints left as the page was held down for viewing. He sensed that the book had had a special meaning to someone and knew that Dr. Miller had lent him something out of the ordinary.

Charley marvelled to himself at how many nice things seemed to be happening to him all of a sudden. He wasn't sure he deserved them, but it really helped to know that people like Dr. Miller and Mr. Bharati were behind you not only with support, but with the kind of generosity he hadn't known since he was a five year old kid at Christmas time. As he moved on to the elevator, Charley felt lucky.

Sri Ramakrishna

CHAPTER TWELVE

A Sweet Dream

Charley was flat on his back with a fever running near 101 degrees. In his dual capacity as an M.D., Dr. Miller had quickly diagnosed Charley's illness as a good old-fashioned case of the flu. He wasn't alone, several others in the hospital had caught it. Tough shit! It was going to delay his discharge for a day or two until he got back on his feet again. What the hell, he thought, it's really not all that bad. The combination of fever and mild medication made him feel sleepy most of the time, and he wasn't in any great discomfort. He "popped" two more of the pills Dr. Miller had prescribed along with several swallows of orange juice. Down the hatch, he thought. Probably nothing more than aspirin and an antihistamine.

Bunching his pillows up under his head, he reached over to his table and picked up the book Dr. Miller had lent him on Ramakrishna. It mentioned Mr. Bharati's teacher several times, and Charley was intrigued by it although as yet he had read only bits and snatches. He had been especially interested when he came to exchanges between Ramakrishna and Narendra, the sometimes doubting and rebellious young man who was later to take the monastic name of Vivekananda. One was the questioning student, brilliant and well educated, the other was the Master, an enlightened country priest with no education to speak of—unlettered, but with a fabulous store of retained knowledge in the oral tradition.

As Aldous Huxley had cautioned in the foreword, much of the thinking and feelings expressed in the book were entirely Indian and Hindu. However, as Huxley had predicted, after a few surprises and bewilderments Charley had begun to find something peculiarly stimulating and instructive about this very strangeness.

Charley began to thumb through the pages. His head was really too fuzzy to read much, he thought. He stopped at

A Sweet Dream

one of the illustrations, a blow-up of an old grainy photograph titled "Sri Ramakrishna in samadhi." He paused to look at it, curious to see a man in the state of samadhi, supposedly united in body, mind and spirit with God. In the picture, Ramakrishna was lightly bearded and smiling. He wasn't what you'd call good looking, but there was an appeal in his face that drew your eyes to it. He was probably around forty years old, with a gap between his two front teeth and a hard to describe focus to his eyes.

Charley looked at other pictures: of a complex of multi-domed temples on the sacred river Ganges, of the strange black goddess Kali whom Ramakrishna worshipped, of Ramakrishna's serene-looking wife, and of many disciples and followers. All from a strange, far away place and time that appealed to Charley's feverish mind.

As he turned the pages, a folded letter slipped from them. Charley smiled. He remembered writing Mr. Bharati immediately after his first session with Dr. Miller. He had thanked him for sending his manuscript copy of the Gita, and as Dr. Miller had suggested had briefly described his experience with the ancient voice in his head that had said so many things similar to the dialogues of Krishna in the Gita. He also mentioned as best he could remember Dr. Miller's reference to Jung's "voice in his head" and his concept of a collective unconscious operating in each of us.

Mr. Bharati, as seemed to be his style, had responded right away. Charley had read and re-read the letter so that he almost knew it by heart when he picked it off the covers where it had fallen and began to read it again:

Dear Charley,
I received your letter today.
I know about Jung's theory of the collective unconscious which has spawned new groups of psychiatrists. Jung had also theories about the prophetic character of dreams. He no doubt enlarged the view of the unconscious.

Truly the unconscious is universal. But beyond this maya, or illusion, is the Reality of God, knowing which a person becomes All, or nothing or whole.

One doesn't go very far by thinking of the unconscious, collective or otherwise. One doesn't go very far through analysis or language.

One has to believe in the Superconscious and approach it through faith and speechlessness, through meditation.

Vivekananda said in one of his lectures that the universe (mind and matter) is like a cobweb and that the mind is like a spider which always has the ability to traverse to any corner of the web. Past, present and future are all in the universal mind—ever present that is. Difficult to imagine though, but a fact substantiated by paranormal perceptions.

Voices are heard from the unconscious—from both aspects of maya, the illusion that causes duality. They are heard from avidya maya, or the maya of ignorance, that consists of anger, passion, and so on, and entangles one in worldliness; and they are heard from vidya maya, or the maya of knowledge, that consists of kindness, purity, unselfishness, and so on, and leads one to liberation. Both belong to the relative world.

Religious literature is replete with instances of voices of both kinds.

Also you will find in the *Gospel of Ramakrishna* how Ramakrishna analyzed the dream of a devotee, whom I presume was M., the narrator, and saw its prophetic nature. I think Ramakrishna interpreted the dream as a symbol of the devotee's crossing the ocean of existence as they say in India with the help of the Guru, the Brahmin.

Dreams bring messages of many kinds. Vivekananda in one of his letters mentions that dreams reveal truths hidden in the different layers of mind.

So your voice really has many precedents in both waking and dream states and is quite authentic.

Thank you for telling me about your experience. I think it was a good one for you and that you must have earned it in one way or another in the past.

                Best wishes,
                K. Bharati

With a sigh, Charley slowly folded the letter and placed it back in the book. He let the book close, too drowsy to read. He felt comfortable in a feverish way, if there is such a state. Presently, before he knew it, he eased off into a delicious sleep.

Charley was in a dreamland. It wasn't a nightmare in Vietnam this time. It was a place he'd never been, like a fairyland. He'd been a passenger on a boat on a broad river shimmering in beautiful moonlight. The boat pulled by oarsmen had docked and left him at the base of wide marble steps leading upwards to a portico on two sides of which, north and south, were two matching rows of temples which appeared to be Indian and mystical in the moonlight. He walked past these temples into a large courtyard where he found two more temples, one very large and in the center with nine domes and gleaming spires surrounding it. He sensed that this central temple had something to do with Kali, the black goddess of creation, preservation and destruction. He vaguely hoped that she was in mode one or two tonight and would protect him. The line "protect us with your auspicious face" ran through his head from Mr. Bharati's meditation tape.

Three sides of the courtyard appeared to be lined with chambers of various kinds. Charley seemed to know where he was going. He went northwest through the courtyard and, walking up a few steps onto a veranda, went through a door to the chamber that stood to the north of the last temple. He noticed upon entering that there was another entrance to the chamber from a semi-circular porch to the west of the room. The semicircular porch overlooked the river which looked serene and mysterious in the moonlight.

The room was lighted and there was a small gathering of men and teenage boys in it. Most of them were dressed in what appeared to be white sheets wrapped around their bodies in various fashions. Charley noticed with some surprise that he was dressed in the same manner, naked from the waist up. He entered the room and bowing slightly saluted, with his hands pressed together in the form of a temple against his heart, the small, thin, extremely delicate man who sat on a couch in the center of the room talking to the surrounding men and youths who sat on the floor. The tiny man acknowledged Charley with a nod and glance with eyes that to Charley seemed illumined with a soft inner light. Good humor seemed to spring from these eyes and appeared in the upturned corners of his mouth. His speech was Bengali, which Charley was pleased to find he could understand with ease. It was of a homely kind with a slight, delightful stammer. His words as he talked held his audience spell-bound by their wealth of spiritual experience, their amusing store of homespun simile and metaphor, their acute power of observation, their bright and subtle humor, and their ceaseless flow of natural wisdom, occasionally spiced with earthiness or sprinkled with "fish water," as he called it.[1]

As Charley seated himself on the floor and folded his legs into the easy posture, he somehow knew he was in the presence of Ramakrishna. Sri Ramakrishna was conversing with an imposing heavy-set man who sported a handsome mustache. Again Charley knew this had to be Girish Ghosh, a born rebel against God, a skeptic, a Bohemian, a drunkard, and the greatest Bengali dramatist of his time. He had plunged into a life of dissipation and had become convinced that religion was only a fraud. But a series of reverses shocked him and he became eager to solve the riddle of life. After crossing paths often with Ramakrishna and being unimpressed, he gradually gave in to an irresistible urge to be with Ramakrishna and became a steadfast devotee. Even so, he continued to drink and often showered Ramakrishna with insults, drank in his presence and took liberties that astounded the other followers. Unable to control and discipline his life, Girish, in an action that illustrates and anticipates many of the Twelve Steps, finally gave Ramakrishna his "power of attorney" and tried to give up all idea of personal responsibility and to surrender himself to Divine Will.

Girish looked to Charley like a battle-scarred sponsor from AA with innumerable benders and drinking bouts under his belt. Guess he really turned things over to his Higher Power, thought Charley, admiring the famous figure who sat talking a short distance away; I sure could use a sponsor like him continued Charley who among other things was having trouble finding someone he felt comfortable and compatible with to be his guide and counsellor in the Twelve Step program.

Returning to the conversation that was already underway, Ramakrishna said to Girish, "You had better argue about God with Narendra and see what he has to say." Girish replied, "Narendra says that God is infinite; we cannot even so much as say that the things or persons we perceive are parts of God. How can Infinity have parts? It cannot."

Ramakrishna responded, "However great and infinite God may be, His Essence can and does manifest itself through man by His mere will. God's Incarnation as a man cannot be explained by analogy. One must feel it for oneself and realize it by direct perception. An analogy can give us only a little glimpse. By touching the horns, legs, or tail of a cow, we in fact touch the cow herself; but for us the essential thing about a cow is her milk, which comes through the udder. The Divine Incarnation is like the udder. God incarnates Himself as man from time to time in order to teach people devotion and divine love."

Girish continued, "Narendra says, 'Is it ever possible to know all of God? He is infinite.'"

With a shrug, Ramakrishna said, "Who can comprehend everything about God? It is not given to man to know any aspect of God, great or small. And what need is there to know everything about God? It is enough if we only realize Him. And we see God Himself if we but see His Incarnation.

Girish Chandra Ghosh

Suppose a person goes to the Ganges and touches its water. He will then say, 'Yes, I have seen and touched the Ganges.' To say this it is not necessary for him to touch the whole length of the river from Hardwar to Gangasagar. (The room rippled with laughter, and Charley thought, ten to one that's the Ganges out there shimmering away in the moonlight.)

"If I touch your feet, surely that is the same as touching you. (More Laughter. Charley thought to himself that it wasn't all that funny. Their sense of humor seemed to be a little different here.) If a person goes to the ocean and touches but a little of its water, he has surely touched the ocean itself. Fire, as an element, exists in all things, but in wood it is present to a greater degree."

Smiling, Girish said, "I am looking for fire. Naturally I want to go to a place where I can get it."

Also smiling, Ramakrishna said, "Yes, fire, as an element, is present more in wood than in any other object. If you seek God, then seek Him in man; He manifests Himself more in man than in any other thing. If you see a man endowed with ecstatic love, mad after God, intoxicated with His love, then know for certain that God has incarnated Himself through that man.

"There is no doubt that God exists in all things; but the manifestations of His Power are different in different beings. The greatest manifestation of His Power is through an Incarnation."

Girish continued the conversation, "Narendra says that God is beyond our words and thought."

Another figure had entered the room and sat down near Girish, next to Ramakrishna. He was an extremely handsome young man nearing twenty years of age. He radiated great physical presence and virility. He had a vivid imagination, deep power of thought and keen intelligence. And he had an extraordinary memory, a love of truth, a passion for purity, a spirit of independence, and a tender heart. Charley knew immediately that this had to be Narendra, the person Girish and Ramakrishna had been talking about and that this young man would later become the legendary Swami Vivekananda who was to bring Indian philosophy to the West near the turn of the century.

Obviously pleased to see Narendra, Ramakrishna turned to Girish and said, "I should like to hear you and Narendra argue about that in English."

The discussion began, but they talked in Bengali, knowing Ramakrishna was joking and knew only a few simple words of English. Narendra said, "God is infinity. How is it possible for us to comprehend Him? He dwells in every human being. It is not the case that He manifests Himself through one person only."

Tenderly, Ramakrishna interrupted, "I quite agree with Narendra. God is everywhere. But then you must remember that there are different manifestations of His Power in different beings. Through different instruments God's Power is manifest in different degrees, greater and smaller. Therefore all men are not equal."

Continuing the argument, Girish said to Narendra, "How do you know that God does not assume a human body?"

Narendra replied, "God is beyond words or thought."

Again, Ramakrishna interjected, "No, that is not true. He can be known by the pure buddhi, which is the same as the Pure Self. The seers of old directly perceived the Pure Self through their pure buddhi."

Girish went on to Narendra, "Unless God Himself teaches men through His human Incarnation, who else will teach them spiritual mysteries? God takes a human body to teach men divine knowledge and divine love. Otherwise, who will teach?"

Narendra spoke back, "Why, God dwells in our own heart; He will certainly teach us from within the heart."

Tenderly Ramakrishna said, "Yes, yes. He will teach us as our Inner Guide."

Gradually Narendra and Girish became involved in a heated discussion. If God is Infinity, how can He have parts?

A Sweet Dream 137

What did Hamilton say? What were the views of Herbert Spencer, of Tyndall, of Huxley? And so forth and so on.

Ramakrishna finally stopped them, saying, "I don't enjoy these discussions. Why should I argue at all? I clearly see that God is everything; He Himself has become all. I see that whatever is, is God. He is everything; again, He is beyond everything. I come to a state in which my mind and intellect merge in the Indivisible. At the sight of Narendra my mind loses itself in the consciousness of the Absolute. (Turning to Girish) What do you say to that?"

Smiling, Girish said, "Why ask me? As if I understood everything except that one point!" (Everyone laughed. Inside jokes again, thought Charley.)

Then Ramakrishna looked at Narendra and said, "As long as a man argues about God, he has not realized Him. You two were arguing. I didn't like it.

"How long does one hear noise and uproar in a house where a big feast is being given? So long as the guests are not seated for the meal. As soon as food is served and people begin to eat, three quarters of the noise disappears. (More laughter.) When dessert is served there is still less noise. But when the guests eat the last course, buttermilk, then one hears nothing but the sound 'soop, sup'. When the meal is over, the guests retire to sleep and all is quiet.

"The nearer you approach to God, the less you reason and argue. When you attain Him, then all sounds—all reasoning and disputing—come to an end. Then you go into samadhi, sleep, into communion with God in silence."[2]

A firm, repeated knocking on the door brought Charley slowly out of his dream world and back to his room in the rehabilitation center. A deep voice said, "Charley man, are you there?" Charley realized it had to be Samson who was getting ready for discharge and called out, "I'm just making it out of bed Samson. Give me about five minutes. I'd like to see you before you check out."

Charley lay back, trying to sort things out in his feverish haze. A beautiful dream, he thought, hating to break the spell he'd been under in that far-off room overlooking the Ganges. I'll tell Dr. Miller about it, but I feel no urgency, no upset, nothing but a wonderful feeling of peace and well-being. For all I know that dream may have been a little like that fair wind of grace I remember Mr. Bharati quoting from Ramakrishna. Would I recognize it if it was? I don't know, I think I might.

As he went to open the door for his caller, Charley fleetingly thought of the black goddess Kali and began to hum softly one of his favorite songs, "That old black magic has me in its spell . . ." Was he slightly delirious? No matter, he felt good about things, and fever or not, was about ready to return to the outside world. He wasn't sure when, how or where he could be certain he'd found a higher power, but he didn't think it was far away, and he knew with help and support from AA, NA, Dr. Miller, Mr. Bharati and his new friends and companions that he could begin to face life without alcohol and drugs. Quite a change in four short weeks, he thought, quite a change.

POSTSCRIPT

"Lead Me from the Unreal to the Real"

. . . from the *Brihadaranyaka Upanishad*

Having read this far, many readers will have surmised that *Twelve Steps from the East* is much closer to fact than fiction. As Mr. Bharati might have remarked to Charley, "Ramakrishna said that even scriptures are a mix of sugar and sand."

While this book is a novel, and must be termed a work of fiction, much of it is either based on autobiographical history or on material drawn from the introduction, verses and comments to be found in *The Bhagavad Gita: A Scripture for the Future* by Sachindra Kumar Majumdar.

It was as I helped Mr. Majumdar, a teacher and friend for more than thirty years, prepare his new work on the *Gita* that *Twelve Steps from the East* took form in the back of my head. As I started putting the novel down on paper, his comments and help in weaving Indian philosophy into the manuscript were invaluable. At times, without intending to do so, he contributed material to the book through our almost daily conversations and correspondence about work in progress or occasionally in answer to questions that I had asked. Thus, I am deeply indebted to Mr. Majumdar whose wealth of Indian philosophy provides so much of the non-fictional foundation for this book.

Another substantial non-fictional portion of the book is to be found in the last two chapters where *The Gospel Of Sri Ramakrishna* as translated into English by Swami Nikhilananda is introduced. The conversation between Ramakrishna, the young Vivekananda and the alcoholic Girish actually took place on March 11, 1885 in Calcutta and was written down afterwards from memory by M., the recorder of the *Gospel*. While it remains substantially intact, I have abbreviated and rearranged the dialogue to make reading a little easier for a first-time Western reader unfamiliar with the *Gospel*. I am very much indebted to the Ramakrishna-Vivekananda Center in New York City for permission to include this material as well as photographs of Swami Vivekananda, Sri Ramakrishna and Girish Chandra Ghosh. The dream sequence that leads into this conversation, though fictional, would be to many of us a welcome one to have.

While it is not all that unusual for alcoholics and other addicts to hear voices, the voice of the *Gita* sounding through Charley's head is a dramatic device used to present pertinent verses of the *Gita* which are then related to the Twelve Steps through the medium of Charley's reactions to them. These reactions are often similar to ones that I have had at one time or another in reading the *Gita* and thus tend to be autobiographically based. They are the honest, to the best of my ability, reactions of a Western mind to a strange and refreshing scripture from the East.

Without violating the AA Tradition of Anonymity, I can say that the setting at the Institute of Pennsylvania Hospital in Philadelphia and Charley's dilemma of lacking a higher power are all too real and familiar to myself and other members of my family. I can also say without exaggeration that many participants in the Strecker Rehabilitation Program of the hospital become discouragingly stalled in the Twelve Step program because they lack belief in a higher power, without which it is impossible to work through the Twelve Steps. It was when we were faced with this dismaying problem that it occurred to me that the message of the *Gita* might provide a new and alternative way of looking at the Twelve Step Program for many troubled people.

Some of the many references to the Twelve Step Program owe credibility to exposure to Al-Anon Family Groups which my wife and I have attended in an attempt to distance ourselves from the problems which addiction creates in a family. As many readers would know, the Twelve Step Program can be applied to any situation in life and is far from restricted to the problems of alcoholics and other addicts.

Probably the most fictionalized part of *Twelve Steps from the East* is chapter four, "The Nightmare". Although I have no first-hand knowledge of the Vietnam War, many Vietnam veterans have ended up with severe drug and alcohol problems brought on by their experience in this conflict. It is my hope that this fictionalization of Krishna's sermon to Arjuna on the battlefield between opposing armies of cousins can offer solace and relief to some of these questioning soldiers.

Wherever Mr. Bharati, the Indian yogi, appears his words are most often actually those of Mr. Majumdar either taken from his book or from letters that he has written to me. (He writes that he feels "shy" when he reads about Mr. Bharati.) When Charley and his friends visit Mr. Bharati in New York City, the apartment scene, meditation and conversation described are similar to those I had with Mr. Majumdar over the course of many years when I was a private student of his in New York City. I'm convinced that my weekly visits with him kept me afloat in the advertising business during this stressful but fascinating period in my life. It was during these years that my interest in the *Gita* developed and took root. Curiously, one of my close business associates at this time was David A. who was a member of AA. Through me, he became interested enough in yoga to remark more than once on the similarity between yoga philosophy and that of the Twelve Steps. This was another factor that supported me in my search for a dramatic way to relate the two without turning people off by preaching or pedantry.

While time and circumstances have been altered, references to Charley's adventures in the advertising business and his musical exploits are drawn from my earlier personal experience in both areas. Family background, the development of the 'Curves', impressions at the Metropolitan Museum of Art, the episode with Sri Agananda, the brief mention of Rabindranath Tagore and his photograph, and much other material pertaining to the practice of yoga are closely related to events in my life and can be considered to be fictionalized nonfiction.

The two psychiatrists and three fellow inmates that appear in the book are pure fiction, although here again much of what they say and do is based on memories about friends, alcoholic and otherwise, from the near and distant past.

Initially I had intended for *Twelve Steps from the East* only to relate the *Gita* to the Twelve Step Program. Instead, the book seemed to take on a life of its own and expanded to a broader perspective of Eastern philosophy. It now includes meditation and many related topics that lead to the final dream sequence with Ramakrishna on the Ganges. If the reader has no more than found it interesting and informative, I will have succeeded and am pleased.

Ralph L. Brockway
March 1991

P.P.S. As this book nears publication, both Mr. Majumdar and I, independent of each other, have had further thoughts about the Twelve Steps.

He writes, "There are 'alcoholics' who are not anonymous—addicts of pleasure and power, as the Gita says in chapter 2. Faith is the cure in both cases. The Twelve Steps are spiritual steps and will lead an addict to further exploration of the spiritual Truth in us all. I think the Twelve Steps will have a good impact on those seeking help in the numerous groups all over."

In my case, it has become clear to me, in full circle, that just as the Indian yogas can help and support practice of the Twelve Steps, the Twelve Steps can help and support practice of the Indian yogas. With little modification, they complement and reinforce each other; indeed, they may even be synergistic. Will the Twelve Steps march East as the Indian yogas come West? Time will tell, as Charley would say.

R.L.B.
January 1992

APPENDIX

Twelve Suggested Steps

1. We admitted we were powerless over alcohol—that our lives had become unmanageable.
2. Came to believe that a Power greater than ourselves could restore us to sanity.
3. Made a decision to turn our will and our lives over to the care of God, *as we understood Him.*
4. Made a searching and fearless moral inventory of ourselves.
5. Admitted to God, to ourselves and to another human being the exact nature of our wrongs.
6. Were entirely ready to have God remove all these defects of character.
7. Humbly asked Him to remove our shortcomings.
8. Made a list of all persons we had harmed, and became willing to make amends to them all.
9. Made direct amends to such people wherever possible, except when to do so would injure them or others.
10. Continued to take personal inventory, and when we were wrong promptly admitted it.
11. Sought through prayer and meditation to improve our conscious contact with God *as we understood Him,* praying only for knowledge of His will for us and the power to carry that out.
12. Having had a spiritual awakening as the result of these steps, we tried to carry this message to alcoholics, and to practice these principles in all our affairs.

The Twelve Steps are reprinted with permission of Alcoholics Anonymous World Services, Inc. Permission to reprint and adapt the Twelve Steps does not mean that A.A. has reviewed or approved the contents of this publication nor that A.A. agrees with the views expressed herein. A.A. is a program of recovery from alcoholism—use of the Twelve Steps in connection with programs and activities which are patterned after A.A., but which address other problems, does not imply otherwise.

NOTES

Chapters 1 and 2

1. The Twelve Steps of Alcoholics Anonymous and Narcotics Anonymous. See Appendix.
2. Indented paragraphs above are selected and adapted from *The Bhagavad Gita: A Scripture for the Future*, chapter 7, "The Yoga of Spirit and Nature," verses 6-30. Translation by S. K. Majumdar. Published by Asian Humanities Press, 1992.
3. Indented paragraphs above are selected and adapted from op. cit., chapter 3, "The Yoga of Action (Karma Yoga)," verses 3-43.

Chapters 4 and 5

1. Indented paragraphs above are selected and adapted from op. cit., chapter 1, "The Yoga of Arjuna's Despondency," verses 26-46.
2. Indented paragraphs above are selected and adapted from op. cit., chapter 2, "The Yoga of Wisdom (Samkhya)," verses 1-72.
3. Indented paragraphs above are selected and adapted from op. cit., chapter 4, "The Yoga of Knowledge (Jnana Yoga)," verses 5-7 and 14-42.

Chapter 6

1. *The Gospel of Sri Ramakrishna* translated by Swami Nikhilananda, page 804. Published by Ramakrishna-Vivekananda Center, New York, copyright 1942 (1984 edition).
2. Mr. Bharati's lecture and answers to questions were extracted (in most part) from various sections of *The Bhagavad Gita: A Scripture for the Future*, by Sachindra Kumar Majumdar. Published by Asian Humanities Press, 1992.

Chapter 7

1. In times past, this has been the spell-casting cry of Indian magicians as they perform their feats of illusion. Chapter XVI, note 1, *The Gospel of Ramakrishna*, as translated into English by Swami Nikhilananda and published by the Ramakrishna-Vivekananda Center of New York, copyright 1942 by Swami Nikhilananda.

Notes

2. Indented paragraphs above are selected and adapted from Majumdar, op. cit., chapter 6, "The Yoga of Meditation," verses 4-47.

Chapter 8

1. Many of Mr. Bharati's remarks in this chapter have been selected and adapted from Majumdar, op. cit., introduction and commentary.

Chapter 9

1. *Fundamentals of Yoga* by Rammurti Mishra, M.D., published by Julian Press 1959.
2. Indented paragraphs above are selected and adapted from *The Bhagavad Gita: A Scripture for the Future,* chapter 9, "The Royal Yoga," verses 1-31, translation by S. K. Mujumdar. Published by Asian Humanities Press, 1992.
3. Ibid., verse 34.

Chapter 10

1. Op. cit., chapter 18, "The Yoga of Liberation," verses 1-11.

Chapter 11

1. Pages 92-93, *New Pathways in Psychology,* Maslow and the Post-Freudian Revolution, by Colin Wilson. A Mentor Book published by New American Library, 1974.
2. Page 183, *Memories, Dreams, Reflections,* by C. G. Jung, Pantheon Books.
3. From *The Gospel of Sri Ramakrishna*, as translated into English by Swami Nikhilananda and published by the Ramakrishna-Vivekananda Center of New York, copyright 1942 by Swami Nikhilananda (1984 edition).
4. Tagore poems are free translations by S. K. Majumdar.

Chapter 12

1. Description, with exception of reference to "fish water" adapted from page 43, Introduction to *The Gospel of Sri Ramakrishna*, as

translated into English by Swami Nikhilananda and published by the Ramakrishna-Vivekananda Center of New York, copyright 1942 by Swami Nikhilananda (1984 edition). Also for descriptions that follow, see pages 51-52 for Girish Ghosh and page 56 for Narendra. Reference to "fish water" is based on a conversation with S. K. Majumdar who said that some of the earthiness or spice of the the original Bengali version was omitted in the English translation.

2. Conversations adapted and reconstructed from pages 725-26, 732-33, 735, chapter 38, "With the Devotees in Calcutta," from *The Gospel of Sri Ramakrishna*, as translated into English by Swami Nikhilananda and published by the Ramakrishna-Vivekananda Center of New York, copyright 1942 by Swami Nikhilananda (1984 edition).